Penguin Books

Marriages

♦

Amy Witting was born in Annandale, an inner suburb of Sydney, in 1918. She attended Sydney University, then taught French and English in State schools. She has published two novels, *The Visit* (Nelson, 1977) and *I For Isobel* (Penguin, 1989), a book of verse, *Travel Diary* (Woodbine Press, 1985), as well as numerous poems and short stories in magazines such as *Quadrant* and the *New Yorker*.

Marriages

◆

AMY WITTING

Penguin Books

Penguin Books Australia Ltd
487 Maroondah Highway, PO Box 257
Ringwood, Victoria, 3134, Australia
Penguin Books Ltd
Harmondsworth, Middlesex, England
Viking Penguin Inc.
40 West 23rd Street, New York, NY 10010, USA
Penguin Books Canada Limited
2801 John Street, Markham, Ontario, Canada, L3R 1B4
Penguin Books (N.Z.) Ltd
182-190 Wairau Road, Auckland 10, New Zealand

Published by Penguin Books Australia, 1990
2 4 6 8 10 9 7 5 3 1

Typeset in 10/11.5 Palatino by Leader Composition Pty. Ltd.
Made and printed in Australia by Australian Print Group, Maryborough, Victoria

National Library of Australia
Cataloguing-in-Publication data:

Witting, Amy, 1918-
Marriages.
ISBN 0 14 012754 2.
I. Title.
A823'.3

The following stories from this collection have been published previously: 'The Survivors' in *Stand* (England), 'Peppercorn Rental' in *Coast to Coast*, 'Goodbye, Ady, Goodbye, Joe' in the *New Yorker*, 'The Man With the Impediment' in *Coast to Coast*, and 'A Bottle of Tears' in *Southerly*.

Contents

♦

The Survivors

♦

It was hot in Len Fuller's shop, but worse outside. At the screen door flies kept buzzing and battering, wanting refuge from the sun, and beyond it one saw the sharp knife-edge of the summer light. Kevin paid for his cigarettes and pocketed his change slowly, leaning against the counter, looking in his mind for a word or two to say to the shopkeeper.

The girl came in carefully, opening the door just wide enough — and that wasn't far — and slipping in quickly to foil the flies. She put her grocery list on the counter and waited.

'Hello, Gloria,' said Kevin. That'll give you a start, said his tone, full of self-contained amusement.

She turned her head and seeing that he was a stranger turned quickly away, leaving the memory of light grey eyes in a small pale face, a child's face with an old pattern of sorrow set in its bones. Not too bad, he thought, looking at the long fair hair that clung wet with sweat to the back of her neck. The cotton dress clung too, so that he could see she had a bit more figure than he had thought at first. No too bad at all.

'Ma says she doesn't like that brand, Mr Fuller.' She spoke with poise and propriety. 'All juice and no fruit, she says. Do you have another brand?'

It was Len Fuller who had told Kevin her name, a couple of days ago, meaning no harm. Now he was sorry. He put the tin of peaches back on the shelf with a bad-tempered thud.

'Tell your Ma I'm not responsible for what's in the tin.'

'She ain't blaming you, Mr Fuller. Just wants to try a different brand, that's all.'

She knew Kevin was there, all right. His mouth stirred to a smile that did not disturb the rest of his regular, neatly upholstered features, but reappeared as a gleam of pleasure in his brown eyes. When the door had shut behind the girl he moved, followed her out to the road and walked behind her along the bottom of the ocean of burning air, not hurrying but gaining on her all the time.

'Hi, Gloria!'

That stirred her, but it didn't surprise her. His smile widened.

'Hi, Gloria!' Now he was walking level with her. 'Carry your bag?'

She shook her head, though the bag of groceries was weighing her down and she drooped in the heat.

He didn't mind the heat just then. The hot, soft dust that rose round his thonged sandals moulding his feet, the sweat at his hairline, the burning streak of sunlight across his shoulders and the shirt clinging wet to his ribs made him more conscious of himself as the object of the girl's attention. Caring no more for the flies than a statue cares for pigeons, he walked slow and complacent beside her and left the next move to her.

'How did you know my name?'

She had meant the question to be severe, but shyness won out over severity.

'Ah, that'd be telling.'

Now she let him take the string bag and began to brush away from her neck the flies that were looking for shelter under her hair.

'Go on. How did you know?'

This time she was sharper, having let the bag go.

'You got nice hair.'

'The flies like it all right.'

'They got good taste.'

For Kevin, that was a flight of fancy, which made him feel inspired. It left her speechless, too. Uncertainly and after too long a pause, she said, 'I don't know you.'

'Well, I know you, don't I? Gloria.'

Now she looked troubled. They were coming to the corner where she would leave the main road.

'Tell you what. You ask me my name and I'll tell you. We'll be square, then.'

At the corner he said, 'Stop a minute,' and she stopped. After all, he had the string bag.

'What's your name then?' she asked.

'Kevin. Kevin Drinan. And now you know.'

Looking back later, with pain and difficulty because looking back did not come easily to him, he thought, 'That's where I made my mistake. Joe Blow I should have said.' But he did not know then how long things were remembered.

With her eyes on the bag, she said, 'You new here?'

'Staying at my uncle's, out at Finney's Corner. Giving a hand on the place.'

'I'll have my bag now, thanks.'

'Come and get it.'

'Oh, give it to me. I got to go home.'

'What's your hurry? Plenty of time.'

She made a pass at the bag, but he swung it away out of her reach.

'Oh, come on. My Ma will see me, and I'll get into trouble.'

Just the same, she was laughing a bit.

'Give it to me, go on. You got to give it to me. I got to go home.'

'Where do you live then?'

'Just down the road there, in the house with the lattice.'

As she spoke, she fixed her eyes on his, keeping them away from the bag. He saw through that and when she lunged he was ready and got both her wrists in one hand.

He laughed at her while she struggled and she laughed too, without knowing why, though she wailed, 'You're hurting me.'

'Keep still then. You're hurting yourself.'

Then she stood still and tried asking again, softer this time.

'Give it to me, please.'

In one of the wrists he was holding, he could feel a pulse leaping like a flea. 'Oh,' he thought, 'I'd give it to you, all right. All right.'

'Promise to come for a walk this evening, then.'

'I wouldn't be let.'

'You don't have to say where you're going. Say you're going to see your girlfriend. Be a sport.'

Gloria didn't have a girlfriend. Young sisters and brothers, a mother who was the nearest thing to a friend she had, and a father to be feared like a bad-tempered dog.

She stood quiet, looking perplexed, her wrists relaxed in his hand.

'Can you whistle?'

Puzzled, she shook her head.

'I can. Like this, see.' He whistled four notes. 'Got it?' He whistled again. 'If you hear me whistling outside your place tonight, you better come out or you don't know what might happen.'

She took the bag and left without answering, but he knew that she would come. What else did she have to do?

When she had gone he considered the problem of filling in the next four hours, calmly, because he was hardened to the emptiness of life. He would miss his lift back to the farm — too bad; the less he saw of that dump, the better. Something to eat wouldn't go astray, though. He didn't bother looking in his pocket — all he had there was the price of a beer and if that went his self-esteem would go with it. Just the same he went to the pub, because that was where the life was, and he struck it lucky, because the pubkeeper wanted a hand in the cellar, and he got a meal and a few drinks and the promise of a bed in exchange for a few hours' work. He might have forgotten all about the girl if it hadn't been for the goodlooking waitress who was eating her dinner in the kitchen when he went to get his. He tried to chat her up but there was nothing doing there. He felt restless then and walked out into the hot, dark night, finding his way without thinking to the side road and the house with the lattice.

When he whistled, she came out so fast that she was there in the dark close to him before he expected her. It gave him a start.

They got clear of the house without talking, and he was still silent when they came to the main road, but she had plenty to say, explaining that she wasn't really coming, only she thought her mother would hear, and he mustn't come round again — all the time leading him away from the road into the thin belt of trees and down to the dry bed of the creek. There they stopped and he got hold of her. She started to squawk and cry but she didn't try to get away, and then he had her down on the bristling grass and was working away for dear life, and her squawking was something different that had to be stopped, so he got his hand over her mouth. It was always like that, the way they went on. It frightened him and he would have liked to get away but it was too late to stop. Stop your bloody screaming, he thought, or perhaps he said it, because she was only whimpering now. Then he forgot her altogether. Ah, ah, ah.

Then all of a sudden she was friendly, though she complained about the mess she was in. 'Look at my dress,' she said, 'what am I going to do?' As if he cared. He thought girls were mad, but he didn't let their madness worry him.

He went back the next night, then the job at the pub ran out and he had to go back to the farm where they weren't pleased to see him, and that was putting it mildly. He stood that for three days, then he got out. His uncle gave him nothing either except a few dollars for his train fare and hard words with it. He went back and tried his luck at the pub again but all he got there was the promise of a bed.

He went out and whistled the girl but this time she didn't come running. He had started to walk away when she came after him and started in on him because he hadn't come before.

That was a laugh. He'd only come now because there was nothing else doing, and he walked straight ahead while she chittered around him like a self-important insect. He thought that at any moment he would lengthen his stride and be rid of her, but the desire that came from having nothing else to do was just as strong, after all, as the desire that came from real need, so he interrupted her to say, irritably, 'You coming down to the creek, or aren't you?'

She shut up then and he slowed down so they were walking together. She kept looking at him sideways, but the look on his face stopped her talking. He liked that. In his depression it was a comfort to be having an effect on somebody, even on a girl he'd had, which was the next thing to nobody at all. As they slithered and scrambled down the dry bank, she put her hand on his arm and he let it stay there, feeling lordly.

They sat down on the grass and he rolled over her and pushed his tongue into her mouth, fierce with boredom and misery. Tonight she wasn't complaining. It annoyed him that she softened every ferocious movement with her yielding and clinging. He had liked it better the first time.

'You coming tomorrow night?'

'No fear. I'm getting out. Getting the train tomorrow.'

That stopped her all right. She was quiet for a long time.

'How long are you going for?'

'Going south. Get a job picking fruit. Nothing doing here.'

'Going for good, do you mean?'

'Be back next year for the shearing.'

Then she flung herself on him, put her arms around his neck and kissed him, pushing close to him, and he was just as scandalised as if a strange woman had jumped him. Gawd, he thought, Gawd, too shocked to push her away. At last he got to his feet, shedding her as he went, and set off for the road, leaving her to scramble after him. When they got to level ground, he said loudly, 'So long', quickened his pace and was gone. He couldn't get out of there fast enough.

It was made up of a lot of things, the magic of the shearing season, and though Kevin didn't know it himself, but cursed his aching back and grumbled about the food and the quarters, the work might be the best part of it — the work and the company. He and Lin were forever talking about the breaks in town and looking forward to them, but sometimes they were a disappointment. There was that first minute, though, when he came into the bar, after he'd had a shower and put on his town clothes, the money in his wallet spreading a feeling of ease and freedom right through him — there was nothing to beat that. He had an idea, with not a drink taken and not a card turned, that he was nobody at all, and he was sorry, in a funny sort of way, to be spoken to and to start being Kev Drinan again, though there was nobody he'd rather be.

He went into the Public and found three of the gang there already, set up with schooners in front of them: George with the sad, wiry face and the line of teeth glistening between his thin lips, Blue Avery and Jack Wrightson. There was nobody else in the bar, so the publican Karl was standing chatting with them.

'You ain't wasting no time,' said Kevin.

'We got none to waste,' said George. 'Karl here's got a message for you, Kev.'

He didn't care for the look on George's face, which was always half a grin and might be a bit more than half at the moment.

'Schooner of old, thanks, Karl.'

As he drew the beer, Karl said, 'Been someone in here looking for you.'

'Is that right?'

'Fellow named Thomas. Roy Thomas. You know him?'

'Never set eyes on him.'

Kevin lifted his glass steadily. He was beginning to see the drift of the conversation and suspected Karl of handling it in a particular way. He was a funny fellow. Known for it.

Sure enough, the glass was right at his mouth and they were all watching him when Karl said, 'Got a daughter, Gloria. You know her?'

The glass never budged and he drank a couple of ounces before he put it down.

'Could do.'

'Some fellow knows her pretty well. Too well, I reckon.'

'It don't have to be me.'

'Well, her father's looking for you, that's all I know. And I think he means trouble.'

'Carrying a shotgun, is he, Karl?' said Jack Wrightson, grinning.

'Not that I saw. Behind his back, maybe.' Giving up the pretence of joking, he added, 'I don't want any trouble in my pub.'

'I'm not aiming to make any trouble. Trouble comes looking for me, that might be different.'

Delivered with insolent calm, this answer inspired visible respect in the other members of the gang. Karl turned away with as much discontent in his face as a publican cares to show.

Kevin had a wonderful time at the crown and anchor game that night, a run of luck that was still running strong in his head when he got back to the hotel, thrust the wallet full of winnings under his pillow and fell asleep on it.

Somebody came to fight him for it, and when he struck out at the thief the room filled with shouting and laughter.

'Look at him. He's a game one.'

'Watch out, now. He's dangerous.'

'Hey. Wake up. Wake up, mate.'

He opened his eyes to the face of his friend Lin, round and grinning like a kid's picture of the sun, with his gold eyetooth shining like another little sun inside it.

'Full of fight, ain't he?'

He sat up in bed, hiding the fury he felt at being handled, and shook himself awake.

'You're in strife, mate. Wanted man.'

There were four of them, the three young men and George, all grinning in spite of the warnings they hurled. Lin offset the seriousness of the situation further by handing him a glass of beer.

'Sitting out on the landing, we was,' said George. 'Jack had got around Karl to open the bar and we was sitting there having a beer, when this fellow comes into the yard, looking up at us, see, and he calls out, "Is Kev Drinan there?" It was on the tip of me tongue to say you wasn't up yet, when it came into me head what Karl was saying yesterday about the girl's father looking for you, so I says, "Haven't laid eyes on Kev Drinan this season. Must be working with another gang," I says. Didn't I? And I look round at the others and they back me up. "You got any idea where he is, then?" So we all shake our heads.' George shook his with a solemnity enlivened by enjoyment. ' "You tell him I'm looking for him, then, if you see him. Thomas is my name," he said. So I was right, wasn't I? That was the name, all right. I says, "If I happen across him, I'll tell him." So he went off, but I ain't saying he's satisfied.'

Lin said, 'You better lay low for a while.'

'Does he know you by sight?'

'Not that I know of.'

The conversation spun a warm cocoon around him: lay low — stay out of sight — ah, it's all talk — I wouldn't be too sure. He lay secure at the centre of it, smiling faintly at the ceiling.

'You're a cool customer,' said George with admiration.

That afternoon, they smuggled him out in Lin's car to the pub at Spiny Creek, all of them laughing, George acting like a two-year-old and wanting him to get down on the floor of the car till they got out of town, but he wouldn't come at that, having a fine feeling for the moment when he would become the butt of the joke, instead of its hero.

That happened, of course. By Sunday afternoon George, tormented by boredom, was nagging at Karl to tell Kevin that the girl's father wanted to see him outside. Foiled there, since Karl refused to treat the affair as a joke, he went to the door of the back room where the poker game was going on, calling out, 'Feller here to see Kev Drinan,' then advancing his savage, delicate clown's face into the room to see Kevin jump and withdrawing it, discomfited by his failure.

'It'll die down,' said Lin, who was watching the game for want of anything better to do. He spoke to console Kevin, but he need not have troubled. The sky could fall on that fellow when he was playing cards and he'd never notice.

It didn't die down, for someone was keeping it alive. The enemy stayed out of sight, but the name Kev Drinan travelled ahead of its owner, had been before him into one little pub outside town and was recognised two weekends later by a stranger in Karl's bar.

'Are you Kev Drinan? I met a friend of yours, Roy Thomas, out at Murrigong. Says he's keeping a lookout for you and he'll see you before the shearing's over.'

It was George that led the laughter, and Kevin kept his countenance, but the situation was beginning to bug him.

'Did he say what he was going to do when he saw me?'

'Nothing to do with me,' said the stranger, turning away.

'He can do plenty,' said Karl, 'seeing that the girl's under age.'

Lin said, 'Gawd,' and round Kevin there was a silence as if a cloak had fallen away and left him naked.

'She never told me she was under age,' he said later to Lin. Nobody else was interested now. They sat on Kevin's bed and smoked, Lin keeping a thoughtful look on his face out of respect for Kevin's difficulty, though he didn't know what good thinking would do.

'Stands to reason, if he was going to the police he would've gone by now. They'd be looking for you, and if they was, well, they would have found you, wouldn't they?'

Angrily, Kevin repeated, 'She never told me she was under age.'

Till now Lin had supposed that the poise he admired in Kevin sprang from worldly wisdom. He looked at him with surprise and sympathy.

'It don't make no difference, mate. Wouldn't even matter if she swore she was twenty. I d'know. Judge might take it into account in the sentence.'

At the word 'sentence' Kevin stirred irritably.

'I tell you, mate, if she's under sixteen and you did her, you've had it. If I was you, I'd run for it. Get the train. That's what I'd do.'

Kevin looked sour and said nothing. The clatter, heat and the grease of the sheds, the fierce competitive movement and the pungent smell of the sheep rose with such power in his mind that Lin's words sounded far away. It was short enough, the season, compared with the empty height of summer and the hungry winter.

'She was ready enough,' he said fiercely.

'It don't make no difference,' said Lin with a little too much patience. 'Ah, forget it. He hasn't been to the police and that's the main thing. He might be after you to marry her, though, if she's gone sixteen. He might be thinking you're more use to him married to her than in jail.'

'I don't see it. If I didn't know.'

'No, it's tough. That the law, though.' For all Lin's sympathy, Kevin heard in his voice the complacency of security. 'Ah, he won't do nothing. Like I said, forget it.'

That was the advice Kevin was waiting for. His face lightened as he said. 'Coming down for a beer?'

He did forget the affair, almost completely, but was haunted now and then by the troubling thought of a small monster, something alive that ought not to be alive, whether it was his own name, travelling out of his reach, or a piece of the past that would not die as it should.

The thing materialised three days later outside the shearers' quarters at Andersons'. Kevin was lying on his bed waiting for the evening meal, holding a comic to the fading daylight that came through a window high in the wall behind him and hearing in the background George with his bookie's cry: 'Stew, five to four on. Sausages, even money. Even money, sausages. Rump steak, a hundred to one.'

Outside, there was an unexpected outcry, and his own name hung on the air with obscenities flowering like rockets around it. Then Mr Anderson's voice sounded, firm and sharp.

'Watch your tongue.'

'Get out of my bloody road. I know the bastard's in there. Drinan! You come out here, you hear me?'

'You're drunk. You're in no state to talk to anyone.'

Lin got up from the next bed, put a foot on a beam and pulled himself up to the window. He nodded to Kevin and stepped down to leave him the place.

Kevin peered down at the enemy: a little puffy fellow with a scalded complexion, weeping eyes and a fat belly pouring over his belt. He was drunk all right, reeling about and flailing with his short arms as he shouted in a voice more powerful than his frame.

'I'll kill the bloody dirty swine. You let me in there. I'll have his balls.'

Kevin sank down from the window and sat on his bed. He seemed calm under the eyes of the others. His mind was a blank.

Mr Anderson's voice sounded. 'I'll hear no suggestions from you in the state you're in. If you have anything to discuss, come back when you're sober.'

Frank called out loudly, 'Drinan's not here!' and the other men took up the cry. 'Not here! Drinan's not here!'

The relief was so great that Kevin couldn't help smiling. It was like a game, him safe and snug in his hideyhole and so close he could have reached out and touched the other man, if it wasn't for the wall.

Frank got up, opened the door just enough, slid out and shut it quickly behind him. The voices began to move away. Whether they were getting around Thomas, or, drunk-like, he'd forgotten what he'd come for, he was whining now instead of shouting, and then the voices died away altogether. Frank came back in. Kevin grinned. He was never the first to speak, but this time it was up to him to lead the joke.

'Christ, that was a close one.'

Nobody answered. He looked round at them but nobody met his eye. Lin said awkwardly, 'Close all right. I thought you were a goner.'

'Sure thing,' said somebody else, but perfunctorily.

Frank said, without friendship. 'Mr Anderson told him you'd go and talk to him. He says he'll drive you over there tomorrow night.'

This thing. You dealt with it and it came back again. You killed it and buried it, and you turned round and there it was.

'What am I supposed to talk about?'

'You'd know that better than I would.'

The other men, lying on their beds, heavy with the fatigue he shared, pretended to pay no attention. He fixed his eye on the old tobacco tin full of hand-rolled butts giving off a cold metallic smell, but it was dark midnight for him and the properties of the day, the drift of comic books and crime magazines, the naked wood of the walls and the pack of dirty playing cards looked fantastic and gave him no reassurance.

'You might as well have let him in.'

'He was drunk enough to get nasty. We don't want any trouble in the sheds.'

Too cocky by half, Frank could be.

'He'll have forgotten all about it in the morning,' he said in a whine of anger.

'You can take a chance on that if you like. If I were you, I'd talk to him before he talks to the police.'

There was that bossy, self-righteous tone in Frank's voice that the others didn't like; perhaps they weren't liking it now, but they showed nothing. It was their silence that beat him.

When Lin said, in a respectful murmur, 'Are you going?' he shrugged, but he knew that he would go.

'You don't have to marry him if you don't want to,' said Gloria's mother as she pierced a sausage and watched a stream of grease spurt from it into the pan.

It was she who had kept the search for Kevin alive. Being an expert in survival, she had kept Gloria safe by finding employment outside the house for her husband's rage. She had jumped between them, driven by fear to desperate jeering. 'Go on, then, tell him about it, will you? What do you mean, you don't know where he is? Haven't started looking either, that I can see. If you was a man you'd find him all right. Play the big fellow around here, oh yes, that's easy.'

She didn't expect for a minute that he'd find Kevin. She had driven him on, feeling confident that he would fail in anything he undertook, unless it was murdering Gloria. And given the smallest bit of help from this Drinan, she would have got away with it, but this fellow was a bigger fool than Roy, and that was saying something. 'Another fool in the family,' she thought bitterly. However, she wasn't referring to her grandchild.

'You want to think about it,' she said, but without confidence, for Roy was as drunk on his success as he had ever been on beer and he was down at the pub reinforcing its effect, so he wouldn't be easy to handle.

'What's come over you?' said Gloria. 'I thought you was all for it.'

Mrs Thomas stopped moving the sausages in the pan to give her a sharp look over her shoulder.

'Get your feet off the rung of that chair, I keep telling you.'

Gloria did not stir. With her heels propped over the rung of the chair, she curled like a thin shell round her swollen belly. Her body was pathetic, but the look on her face was maddening. She had got off too easy and now she had a headful of silly notions. The word 'marriage' had hold of her, and if she only knew what it meant, if you could ever tell them anything . . .

'If you don't want to do it, nobody can make you,' she said, with a shabby idea of handing over responsibility.

'And let Kevin go to jail, I suppose,' said Gloria, handing it smartly back again.

I don't know why you care about him, thought the mother. He don't care much about you. But she didn't say it, out of pity, thinking what the poor little devil had in front of her.

'What about Dad, anyhow? I'm not going to stick around here forever putting up with his abusing and threatening. It's been bad enough having to run and hide and putting up with what he says about Kev.'

'We don't know much about him and what we do know ain't much good.'

Gloria met this with a closed, superior look, just as if Kevin had been turning up every Saturday night to take her to the pictures.

'Go and call the kids for their tea,' her mother said, banging the lid on to a saucepan in a fit of temper that sent Gloria pretty promptly to the door, calling out, 'Mi-ike! Charley! You're wanted!'

Kevin was determined not to marry her. He meant to use the power of silence. He had sat through enough diatribes, staring ahead of him, closing his ears, not caring. He had this great power of not caring, withdrawing inside himself, waiting them out; when he could, he walked away and when he couldn't he sat it out. It had always worked before and it would work this time. So he had the dead look on his face already, from resisting in his mind, when he got out of Mr Anderson's car outside the house, but the father was too pleased with himself, fairly quivering with triumph, to pay any attention. At the sight of him Kevin went deeper into his own thoughts, where absolute resistance welled steady and quiet. His mouth sagged slightly, his eyes brooded. When he followed the father into the dining room and he saw the mother get a real shock at the sight of him, his face took on a sheen of satisfaction without moving a muscle.

'Well, here's your son-in-law,' the drunk was shouting.

She gave him a scared look that made him feel secure in spite of everything.

'Take a seat. Go on. Sit down.'

They all sat at the table and the shouting started.

'Well, when's it going to be, eh? No use sitting there like a bloody image. That ain't going to do you any good. When's the wedding, eh?'

Kevin, facing the door, was staring straight ahead of him, but he was aware of the fidgeting, worried mother getting up courage to speak and he was giving her time.

He wasn't thinking about the girl at all, words like son-in-law and wedding coming at him like fists from nowhere, and there she was in the doorway, the past on her face and the future in her great belly, and it shattered him, for he didn't give thought to either but travelled in the lighted cabin of the moment.

'Come on, now. You know the score. You'll be inside looking out, mate, unless you do the right thing and do it fast.'

With his eyes on the girl, he stammered, 'I can't get married. Got nowhere to take a wife.'

'You should've thought of that before. I'm not having any bastards in this family, do you hear me? Or you'll pay for it if I do. In jail you'll pay for it. So make up your mind. What's it going to be?' He was winning and he knew it, his voice twanging with triumph like the strings of a hideous guitar.

'Got to start at new sheds Monday.' Kevin sounded sulky and helpless now.

The mother opened her mouth, but she hardly got a word out.

'You get out. Go on, out. Go and put a cup of tea on.'

The girl hadn't said anything. She stood there with her eye on him, and now she came silently and took the chair next to him. It was a sign to him that he was beaten.

Oh, Gawd, the mother thought, but young girls were silly. There he was with a face like cheese and looking as if he wished the ground would swallow him up and she looked at him like she was expecting love-talk.

No use talking to her, no use talking to anyone. The mother was full of guilt and misery as she stood watching the kettle on the stove, and still she didn't see what else she could have done. The most you could do about trouble, it seemed, was put it off as long as you could.

Gloria waited with her father and mother in front of the church, which stood isolated on the highway that served as the town's main street. The church was a small wooden building, painted with a dignified lack of pretension in the colours of dust and raw wood. The mother, aiming at neatness as a tribute to solemnity, had polished her shoes, put a new ribbon on her hat, set her hair and pressed her good dress. Having a true sense of occasion, she would not have done better if she could. Gloria had a new dress that made her furiously sulky. She glowered, looking down the road along which Kevin would come.

'Not my fault you're getting married in a maternity dress. You're the one that seen to that.'

Her mother didn't understand. The important thing was that Kev should look at her. He hadn't looked at her yet and when he did everything was going to be all right. Surely, when they faced each other in the church, when the minister was marrying them, he would have to look? For the occasion she needed a miraculous dress that would make her as she used to be, and here she stood in this great pink bag, the hem not even straight.

'Could have done a bit better than this,' she muttered.

At least she had got that silly look off her face that would get her murdered one of these days. Just as the mother was telling herself so, back came the look again. Roy, who had been fixing his steady, narrowed gaze at the length of the road, relaxed with a smirk of triumph. The bridegroom was coming.

The mother turned and faced the road. A friend with him, and both of them as full as boots. They paused ten yards away on the other side of the church. The bullet-headed best man was grinning, silly with drink, his golden eyetooth shining as he came towards them.

'Pleased to meet you. Pleased to meet you. Very happy occasion. How do you do?'

In the silence that met him, he realised he was alone. He looked round and saw that Kev had stayed where he was, uttered a wild giggle and turned back. Kevin took no notice either of his going or his returning but stood wrapped in a haze of alcohol, wearing a gentle, dreamy air.

Just as the minister's car was coming, he whispered in his friend's ear and they disappeared round the side of the church with Roy after them.

They were only going to the outhouse, after all.

Embarrassed, the mother offered the minister a writhing smile. He came and took her hand with a politeness that approached affection, and that made her feel worse than anything up to now. The effort should have come from somewhere else; with him it was only religion, when all was said and done, and the kindness in his face was desolating, because you saw your need for it.

The men came back with the father worrying at their heels like a sheepdog and the best man's face pinned in a silly smirk which the mother tried not to see. She had endured great injuries and forgotten them, but she remembered that smirk with resentment till she died.

It was a consolation to find that the words of the marriage service were the same as ever. The mother wouldn't have been surprised if there had been a special, humiliating version for these circumstances, but the words came in their old order, sober and sustaining, and caused her to hope that things might after all go well. If only the pair of them was really listening.

The bride's father made a speech in the road outside the church.

'Now piss off, you two. And don't come back.' As they stood undecided, the words producing no change in the bridegroom's gentle, stupefied expression, he roared, 'Piss off, you hear. Get going.'

The bridal party began to move off towards the pub, farewelled by a moan of dismay from the mother that would have been ridiculous if it had been intended for anyone's ears.

The bridegroom was moving fast, so that the bride had to scurry to keep up with him, and when she did she was still alone. Lin walked beside them persevering with a smile that kept fading. He liked to think that life was a joke, but he had trouble fitting Gloria's father to his theory.

'Gawd,' he said with awe. 'Your old man, eh? Gawd.'

Mrs Drinan, Mrs Drinan, Mrs Drinan, she was thinking. Say Mrs Drinan a hundred times and everything will be all right. She gave Lin an abstracted look that did nothing for him. It was too long since he had had a drink, besides, and he was sliding into depression when they came within earshot of the cheering Saturday afternoon clamour of the pub.

'Well, let's go and have a beer. Celebrate, eh?'

Gloria said, 'What about me?'

She didn't weep easily, but the circumstances were trying.

'Well, we'll go to the Ladies' Parlour, then.'

'I can't go into the pub at all. I'm under age.'

'Well.' Lin could work his brain no further and Kevin still seemed to be miles away.

'I suppose I can sit in the yard. There's a seat there under the tree. So long as you can put up with the flies.'

'They don't drink much,' he said, and her face lit with pleasure at the joke.

That was enough to cheer Lin. It never took much. She led them through a side gate into the pub yard, where there was a picnic table and benches of wood weathered to the colour of iron and sprinkled with shade from a tall gumtree.

'My shout.'

Lin left them sitting at one of the benches, Kevin with his soft, stupid gaze set on the ground and the girl with a tight little smile, and that was exactly how they were when he got back. The girl looked a proper freak in the pink cotton dress that hung loose everywhere else and curved smooth over her big round belly, and the rest of her so skinny. Not what you'd call a girl at all. It made Lin feel comfortable with her.

'Here you are, Tiger.'

He sat down opposite her. The beer he had put in front of Kevin was half gone already. Before he touched his own, he poured a dribble of it into her lemonade.

'Got to have a drink on your wedding day.'

Wrong thing to say. There was Kev like turned into lead and heavy enough to sink into the ground. But the girl played up to him and made a funny little face, sipping it. You could see her asking herself what she thought of it, so he poured in a little more, and then more. They got a real giggle out of it, considering they were sitting at the same table with what you might call a dead man, except for his thirst. Kev had drunk his beer in two goes and now he was sitting glooming behind the empty glass.

His turn to buy, thought Lin, spinning out the game, pouring so much into her glass this time that she got a real taste of the beer, screwed up her little monkeyface and said, 'Good lemonade spoilt.'

That was the last mouthful of beer he had poured into her glass, so, playing for time, he took a mouthful from hers, rolled the sweetish shandy round his mouth with a horrible grimace, spat it out on the ground and said, 'Bloody good beer spoilt, you mean.'

She really laughed, she wasn't putting it on. She was a caution. One of his own mob.

It must be the first time since he'd known him that Kev hadn't been willing to stand his turn. Look at the girl though and the fix she was in, and she could still raise a laugh. Lin gathered the glasses, saying, 'Same again?' This was the last one, anyhow. They had a long way to go.

'See if my Dad's in there, will you? I want to go home and get some things.'

'Don't worry. If he's in there, I won't wait. I'll come running. I'll go for my life.'

'Go on. I bet you'd wait and get your beer.'

'Depends. If he had his back to me, I might risk it, but I'd be quick about it, I can tell you.'

'Oh, go on. You ain't frightened of much, I bet. Anyway, Dad won't take any notice. So long as he's got his beer, that's all he cares about.'

'Well, here goes. If I'm not back in two hours, come and get me.'

'No fear.'

Looking round the bar, Lin saw the thick soft neck and the pink ears of Roy Thomas who was shouting away in some argument above the noise of the race commentary. The girl was right: there wasn't much danger there. Lin thought, if Kevin didn't have such a case of them, he'd be enjoying this. It was just the sort of thing that gave him a laugh. And then, it wasn't the kid's fault, was it? Not any more than Kev's, anyhow.

He got out unobserved and coming back across the yard he hunched his shoulders, looking cowed and putting on a real clown's act for the girl.

'He's in there, is he?'

'He sure is. Didn't see me, though. We better make this the last. You got to get your things and we got a long way to go.'

Kevin met that with a look of deep rage that startled them both. Having drunk the first beer so fast, he took this one as if he had a bet to make it last an hour. Lin and the girl sat it out quietly for twenty minutes, then he gave her the nod to get up and they walked to the car and waited for him there. That did the trick. He came after them — in his own time, but he came.

Next time one of the gang got married and wanted a pal to stand by, it wasn't going to be Lin.

If Lin had only heard about that wedding cake wilting under the muslin cloth at Thomases' while they were down at the pub, he would have thought it a very funny joke. Seeing it was different. It wasn't a very showy cake, and only the eyes of Gloria's skinny fair-haired brothers and sisters, directed at it from various heights around the table, showed that it was anything special. Gloria's mother knew how far she could aspire without making herself ridiculous and was besides quite indifferent to the neglect that met her efforts. It was the dignity of that indifference that daunted Lin. He found himself embarrassed by the behaviour of Kevin, which drew not one sidelong glance from the others — Saturday afternoon was the time for men to sit swaying from the hips, looking dazed, saying nothing — and to make up for it he tried to be jolly, stuffed his mouth with cake, praised it and blew wet morsels on the tablecloth, while the mother, with worry drawing her face like a headache, said to Gloria, 'You got to watch the real hot weather and cover everything from the flies. And see it gets enough to drink. You got to give it boiled water as well as milk. You boil it up in the morning and keep it in a jug with a cover over it. Don't give it to him too cold though or you'll give him the colic.'

'All right. I know, Ma.'

Gloria, who had been so patient at the pub, looked bad-tempered now. She had given up any idea of shining as a bride but she still didn't want to share the day with the lively load in her belly. She had made a vague appointment with it for a day in the future but she had other things to think about just now.

'You know. You know everything, I suppose,' the mother said angrily.

In a minute she was off again. 'If the heat's real bad you wet the mosquito net before you put it over him. Keep on wetting it, that'll keep him cool. Don't go off in a dream and forget about it, and don't put any clothes on him if it's that hot. Just lie him on his napkin.'

'Well, we better be going,' said Lin. 'Got a way to go.'

'You write and let me know. Don't take too much notice of your father. He's just . . .' She didn't finish the sentence but with a sour look at the young men got to her feet, saying, 'I packed your things.' Buggered if I'm going to carry them, thought Lin, wounded by the look, but when the mother brought out a big battered suitcase with a strap round it and a couple of paper bags, Kev got up and walked to the car without even a look at them, so Lin came after him loaded and looking like a real Charlie, telling himself he would never get into anything like this again.

Even at the door, the mother was still giving advice and had enough in stock to keep them there till midnight. Lin got the engine running, then gave a toot on the horn that brought Gloria scurrying to take her place in the back seat.

When they started off for Sotherns' Kevin was sitting beside him like a block of wood, but little by little he was creeping out of his bolthole of drunkenness and just before they got to the turnoff for Sotherns' he said, quiet and sober, 'Keep straight on to the next turnoff. Going out to my uncle's.'

'Well, thanks for letting me know,' thought Lin. He wondered if the kid knew where she was going, then he pounced on that uneasy thought and squashed it like a running insect. He should mind his own bloody business. Not his affair whether she knew or not, or how she felt about it.

It was getting dark when they stopped in the road outside the farmhouse. This time Kevin moved fast, jumped out, opened the back door and threw the girl's bags out, saying, 'You get out here. Go on, get.'

She got out, but then she hung back keeping her eyes on him.

'Go on. Get moving.'

He was in a temper, all right, but the fury in his voice was put on to frighten her away. She stood still, her peaky little face shining like bone in the half-light. Someone in the house had heard the car. A door opened and showed the outline of a short, stout woman on a background of yellow lamplight.

'Get,' he repeated. He climbed in beside Lin again and said urgently, 'Get going.'

Then for a moment nobody moved. The stout woman paused in the doorway, the girl stood watching them beside the car and Lin in the driver's seat found it impossible to stir.

The woman came out of the house, calling as she came, 'Who's that?'

Kevin spoke in Lin's ear, this time with a bit of a laugh, 'Quick. Get going.'

Lin sat staring at the dashboard as if he had forgotten how to start a car. This was a hell of a day, with the beer wearing off and leaving him cold and sour with a headache knocking gently at his forehead. Should have got a couple of bottles at the pub.

He muttered, 'We got time,' and then felt the air going out of Kevin, caught the edge of his puzzled stare and felt just as puzzled, and ashamed of himself as well.

The woman walked past Gloria towards Kevin. He got out of the car as if there was some way of warding her off.

'Oh, it's you, is it? What the hell do you think you're doing? You're not coming here, I can tell you that. Your uncle's had enough of you, loafing about eating your head off.'

The indignation that possessed the woman was almost too much for her small fleshy body to contain. It sprang and quivered as she shouted.

Desperation made Kevin shout too. 'It's not me. It's the girl. She's got nowhere to go. Her father threw her out.'

She turned round to look at Gloria and said, 'Looks as if he had his reasons, too. Like your bloody hide trying to dump your girlfriends on us, got enough to do to feed our own kids not going to be landed with your bastards don't you think it for a minute. Get going.' She scurried round to get between the girl and the house, looking like something out of the circus though Lin never felt less like laughing, then she started to dog her into the car step by step, face stuck out like a bum and yelling, 'Get out of here, do you hear me? You dirty trollop.'

Lin muttered, 'Can't help hearing you, Ma.' It was so much like a row in a pub that it was terrible to be sober.

Kevin got back in and slammed the door. The girl picked up her suitcase and heaved it into the back seat, then she came scrambling after it, carrying the paper bags.

The woman's battle cry turned into a song of triumph.

'Been the same ever since you was born, you bloody lazy no-hoper, coming here taking the food out of decent people's mouths and never a tap of work. Never want to set eyes on you again you thieving loafer.'

A cluster of children who had been visible for some time in the lighted doorway advanced now and stood listening respectfully a short distance away.

'Oh, for Christ's sake,' Kevin muttered.

Lin started the car, but he had to turn and drive past her again, the fountain of abuse playing triumphantly as they passed.

What with getting drunk and sobering up, taking this trip for nothing and having the long drive back to Sotherns' ahead of him, Lin found this day too long for his mind to measure. He was troubled by the pangs of an empty belly and a full bladder and depressed by the disgrace of having let Kevin down. He didn't know why he'd done that. When Kevin said, 'Quick. Get going,' his hands hadn't moved and he didn't know why.

The road ran for miles through a treeless region. It was fairly dark now, and when they came to a group of spindly trees that offered a conventional idea of shelter he stopped the car, walked across and relieved himself behind them without worrying too much about the girl. Kevin came after him and they stood there crossing swords without speaking. Kevin was shirty with him and no wonder.

There was something else nagging at him, more than hunger or guilt, with the irritation of a word on the tip of his tongue but out of memory's reach. He thought, if he could remember it he would cheer up.

'If Sotherns' don't give her a bed, we'll borrow a couple of blankets and she can doss down in the car.'

He felt better after he said that. It was weird: like there was a fire somewhere on a cold night, you didn't know where and came near it accidentally, feeling the warmth of it, then next minute in the cold again.

The hell with that. He shut his mind to what he didn't understand and told himself that women were to blame for the lot: his hunger, his headache, Kevin's sulks, the lot. Where you had women, you had trouble.

Mr Sothern answered the knock at the door, but when he saw Gloria, looking saint-like from tiredness and hunger, he called, 'Josie! Come here a minute,' and his tall, calm-faced wife appeared, a being so alien to the young men that they hung back, too shy to speak.

There was no need to say anything. Mrs Sothern drew Gloria inside as if she was rescuing her from them. 'You poor little thing. Now you mustn't cry. You're tired out, aren't you?'

Mr Sothern picked up Gloria's luggage and followed them in. Kevin and Lin drove to the quarters to park the car and went to the kitchen looking for something to eat. When they came into the lighted room, Lin noticed that Kevin was wearing a cheerful little smirk. He bounced back fast, all right, the old Kev.

Mrs Sothern drove Gloria to town next morning, took her to the doctor and left her at a friend's house. It was just as well, for the baby boy was born four days later. Mr Sothern came to the quarters to give the news, bringing a quart of scotch to wet the baby's head.

Kevin was squatting on his heels playing poker with three of the others in the space between the door and the first of the beds. He had just discarded three cards — actually his hand was king high but he had kept the nine of spades as well as the king; no point in telling the others his business — and Jack was dealing again when Mr Sothern came in. He never got to look at his cards.

'Well,' said Mr Sothern, 'you're a father. It's a boy. Six pounds, two ounces. Born at five o'clock. He's no heavyweight but he's healthy, the doctor says. Your wife's very well.'

The other men were slapping Kevin on the back, with goodwill but too heartily, as if he was the baby and they were smacking him to start him breathing.

'Good on you, mate!' 'A boy, eh?' 'Teapot!' 'Good for you!' 'Bring up your glasses,' said Mr Sothern.

The cards were trampled and scattered. Kevin might have brought a flush to those spades. He felt it in his bones that he had. He'd never know now.

Blind Freddie would have known she was under age, thought Lin. More like twelve than sixteen. Whenever Kevin spoke to him the thought came and blocked his answer, turning it into a vague mumble that put an end to conversation.

The night before they were paid off at Sotherns', Frank caught him crossing the yard and said, 'Lin, I'd like a word with you in private.'

Lin said warily, 'This is as private as you'll get.'

'About Kevin's wife. The men have put a bit of money together for her and the baby. We want you to give it to her.'

'Why me?' Lin was surly. Wasn't he Kevin's mate?

'You're the only one who knows her. And it's for her and the baby, you understand. You could explain to her. It'd come better from you.'

Fair enough. It was their money; they didn't want to see it go across the board at the crown and anchor. It shook him though, to see what they all thought of Kev. He couldn't say that they were wrong. No saying that they were right, either. He put the money in his pocket but he thought he might tell Kev about it just the same.

They got into town about five o'clock the next day.

'You going up to the hospital?' Lin asked carelessly as they went up the pub stairs together.

The look on Kev.

'What the hell for?' he asked, each word separate, and spitting them out as if they were poison.

Oh, all right. All right. Lin was aware of the bulky envelope in his inside pocket. He'd take it up to her then. One thing, there wasn't any chance of running into Kev.

Kevin went to the pictures first and then to the crown and anchor where he had a bit of luck, enough to cheer him up. He got in at two in the morning and woke up late and feeling fine. He got dressed and went down to the bar looking for Lin, to have a beer before lunch. Lin wasn't there. Jack and Blue and George were just finishing a beer. Jack said, 'Well, here's the new father. We'll have to have a drink on that. Same again, all round, Karl. And have one yourself. Special occasion.'

George raised his glass and said, 'Here's to you, Dad.'

Kevin turned on George the cold furious look that used once to bring silence. They laughed. They knew now that he was harmless.

Jack pushed the beer across to him, still grinning.

'Better drink up, Poppa,' George said pulling the lion's tail.

'Enjoy yourself while you can,' said Jack, winking at Karl.

'Sure enough.' Even Karl was grinning. 'Soon you'll be walking the floor with him at three in the morning while he cuts his teeth.'

Meekly he drank his beer, allowing the look of rage to dissolve slowly into vagueness.

A fly in a web would know his feelings.

Sitting up in bed, pale but cocky, with a shrunken cardigan over her cotton nightdress, she looked as young as ever. Younger.

'Hi, Lin.'

'Hi. I got something for you.'

'From Kev? Didn't he get in?'

'Yeah, he got in. The whole gang's in. Finished at Sotherns'. No, it ain't from Kev. It's from the gang.'

He put the envelope in her lap and she peeked at the wad of notes.

'Gor. Ain't that nice of them.' She stared with awe at the envelope.

'Listen. What they want. They want you to put the money away. For the baby, like. I mean,' — here it came, against his deepest feelings — 'they'd just as soon you didn't say anything about it to Kev.'

There was a long silence while he allowed her to frown over that.

'What I mean is. What they think. Kev's a gambler. You couldn't talk sense to him while he's playing cards. He might take the money and think he was doing you a favour, thinking he'd bring it back double.' That sounded hollow. He never did know much what Kev was thinking, but he doubted if doing favours came into it.

She had been listening carefully and now that he had finished she nodded without any fuss and put the envelope under her pillow.

A nurse pushed a rumbling trolley into the room. When she stopped beside Gloria's bed to put a glass of orange juice on the bed-table she gave Lin such a dirty look that he and Gloria got the giggles and couldn't stop.

'Thinks you're it, don't she?' Gloria snuffled away tears of laughter, then joyful pride took her face over entirely.

'You seen him?'

He shook his head.

'Oh, go on. Go and have a look on the way out. The nurse'll show you. He's lovely, he really is.'

'Get me arrested, you will.' At this they crumpled again.

'Go on. Have a look at him, do.'

'Garn. I bet he's as ugly as sin.'

'No, he ain't. He's cute.'

'When do you get out of here?'

'Wednesday. Mrs Marsh is coming to get me. She's Mrs Sothern's friend. She's lovely. I can go and stay at the pub and do a bit of work for me keep. Just helping with the breakfasts and the teas. People are real nice. Lin . . .'

'Yeah?'

'He ain't coming, is he?'

'Search me. Doesn't tell me everything he does.'

That told her though, all right. Lin wished himself anywhere else, for the minute, and wondered with anger how he came to be in this spot. Always the mug, he said to himself, looking at her with a painful fixed grin.

'Well thanks for coming. And the money. That was lovely.' She perked up all at once. 'Don't forget to have a look at him.'

The following Monday the men started work at Wrights'. It was out of sight out of mind with the girl and the baby. George tried to get some fun out of calling Kevin Daddy, but he gave it up as Kevin refused to be drawn. Lin didn't say a word about it. He stayed close to Kevin and they chatted along quietly about this and that, mostly good times they'd had and funny things that had happened. They weren't good sheds at Wrights' and the food was terrible, but Lin liked the spell they had there. It was the last in the district. After this, they moved south-east.

They cleaned up late on Friday and checked in at the pub early Saturday morning. Karl's wife Mona was handing out the room keys.

'I've moved you into 16 with Gloria, Kevin. It's a double with room for a cot. I've moved in an old cot that you're welcome to

. . . Don't mention it,' she called after him furiously.

'Hasn't settled down yet, Ma,' said George. 'Still got the honeymoon jitters.'

'You mind who you're calling Ma.'

In the corridor Kevin walked into Frank who was coming from the bar with Karl.

'Couple of bills here, Kevin, that you might as well settle out of your cheque. As we're moving on.'

He looked mild and unbelieving at the two envelopes Karl held out to him.

'Do you have a bank account here? I didn't think so. Karl can cash your cheque for you and make a couple out. That'll be the best way.' Pretending to be helpful. Moving in on him. Living his life for him. A man would have done better to go to jail. It was a life sentence. For twenty minutes, a life sentence.

Between the beds in room 16 there was a cot with a teddybear propped up in one corner and underneath it a baby bath and a potty, both in blue plastic. Kevin showered and changed and got out fast. The less time he spent there, the better he'd be pleased. He went down to the bar and had a pint with the flies, spinning it out till a couple of the others came in. He had a few with them. When he went across the yard to the Gents before lunch he saw a canvas crib near the kitchen door and seeing was as sharp as touching, but he was insulated by then.

No Gloria in the dining room. She must be eating in the kitchen. She was laying low, he thought, and that restored some of his self-respect.

In the afternoon they played poker and all the time he was conscious of having less money than the others. It didn't affect his play — he always played cards as if his back was to the wall and he came out ahead, but he felt it.

When the game broke up he took his winnings and joined Lin at the bar.

'What are you doing this evening?' he asked while Karl served him a pint.

Lin was about to say that he thought he'd give the girls a treat and go to the dance, but sentiment stopped him. He and Kev

had always gone to the dance together, and this might be an
indirect plea for his company.

'Dunno. Haven't thought about it.'

'What about coming to the dance, then?'

Lin had a funny expression on his face as if he was trying to
look two ways at once.

'Might go out to Spiny and have a couple of beers with old
Walt. Seeing as we won't be back for a while.'

Kevin's face tightened with temper. A new girl, that was
what he needed. He wanted to go to the dance and pick up a
new girl, somebody with real class. Not just for the night,
either.

It was no use going without Lin. They were hard cases, the
town girls at the local dance, and it was Lin who knew how to
chat them up. Kevin tagged along and did all right, better than
Lin sometimes, but he was no good by himself.

They went out to Spiny Creek but it wasn't much of an
evening. Walt was kept busy because the cricket team was in.
The cricketers were having a fine time but the joy didn't spread
as far as Lin and Kevin. They dragged it out till closing time and
they ended up looking in at the dance when they got back to
town but it was too late to do any good then.

When Kevin got back to the room she was awake feeding the
baby and she stared at him, all eyes, not saying anything. The
look he gave her made her duck her head as if he had raised his
fist. That made him feel a bit better.

Karl and Mona made such a fuss of the baby that they would
probably have given Gloria a permanent job to keep it there.
Kevin wanted Gloria to ask them but he couldn't speak to her,
the silence between them having set as hard as steel. He always
knew what she was doing in spite of that because she told the
baby, chatting to it in an even quiet voice as if she was talking to
herself. Like a bloody madwoman.

When he woke up, the morning they were leaving for Willow
Creek, she was standing at the dressing table doing her hair up
and talking to the waving legs on the bed. 'Don't mess up your
new suit now that Auntie Mona give you. You're going down to
stay with her while I put the stuff in the car. You be good now

and no yelling. Come on, then, we got a lot to do.'

All the stuff was gone when he came back from the bathroom, so he knew what to expect, but the situation hit him just the same when he came out into the hotel yard. Mona was standing by the car holding the baby while Lin and Gloria, as thick as thieves, were trying to pack the boot of the car.

'Try the crib in the boot,' said Mona,' and put the bath on the back seat. Put the pillow in it and you can lie him in it. You'll have a nice sleep then, won't you, pet?'

'A travelling circus, this is,' Lin growled. 'All because of you, mate.' He threw a punch in the baby's direction, but it was Kevin who felt the jolt of it. When Lin said, shortly, 'Come and give a hand with this stuff, Kev,' he went unresisting, and all the way to Willow Creek he sat pensive, too discouraged to be sullen.

Raking the ashes of his temper for a little life-giving warmth he thought of the scene at the car. Everything about it annoyed him: the sunlight, the silly look on Mona's face when she talked to the baby, the tone of Lin's voice and the sight of Gloria so pleased with herself and done up to the nines. She had a new dress on and new sandals too. Where the hell did she get the money for new clothes?

The question was so interesting that he repeated it in a different tone. Where did she get it then? From her mother? Not likely. The old girl wouldn't have two cents to rub together. From Karl and Mona? What a laugh. Her board, she was working for, and Mona had made a sharp remark or two about that. Not to Gloria, of course. To him. Minding his business, like everybody else. The bath and the teddybear — who paid for all that? He meant to keep a good lookout till he found out.

At Willow Creek, remembering the mean note in Lin's voice, he unpacked the car without waiting to be told and stacked the stuff in the lobby outside the office. Gloria waited to talk to the pubkeeper's wife and he waited with her though he resented it, the woman's indifferent glance marrying them again as he stood there.

'Do you need any extra help in the kitchen? I want to earn my keep if I can.'

'I could do with someone full-time to do the rooms. You don't look very strong, though.'

'I'm wiry.'

'How old are you?'

She lied, 'Seventeen.'

'Are you feeding the baby yourself? I think it might be too much for you.' Harried and listless as the woman was, she smiled when she looked at the baby. 'Well, every little helps. We'll see how it works out. How long are you staying?'

Gloria looked at Kevin, who had to mutter, 'Five weeks.'

'But the men will be at the sheds most of the time.'

They had almost had a conversation, and he still didn't know if she was going to earn money. She was like a spider, tossing her soft, sticky threads round him, and the whole world helped her at it. Soon, he knew, he would have to give in.

The country round Willow Creek was livelier than the West. They went to Thompsons' first, six miles from Pike's Crossing where Dan Bryan kept the pub and his daughter Moira ran the bar. The gang was known there. Lin and Kevin drove over the first night and found it just the same as last year, quiet and pleasant, with one or two men from the farms round about talking shop over a pint and Moira behind the bar with her knitting.

'Hello, you two. That's another year gone then.' She set down her knitting and took their order.

'That's right. You don't look a day older, though.'

'Thanks.' Moira drew their beer without smiling.

'That the same old pullover you was knitting last year, Moira?' asked Lin.

'Have to do something to pass the time. I can't travel round like you lot.'

'There ain't so much to travelling around,' said Kevin. 'Not when you've got a nice little spot like this. You don't want a barman, do you? Permanent, live in.'

Moira couldn't count the number of times she'd heard that one. Some of them had meant it, too. She had waited a long time for a man who would offer to take her away from the bar, but they always wanted to join her there.

'See enough of men from where I'm standing, thanks.'

Kevin didn't leave it at that. Next time they ordered, he said, bright-eyed and with the teasing look that brought his face alive, 'Come on, Moira. What have you got against men? We ain't such a bad lot.'

Looking downwards, Moira communicated her opinion of men to the tap of the beer pump. Delighted to see Kevin himself again, Lin said, 'We ain't all the same, you know. You meet one or two that's no good and you take it out on the rest of us. Is that a fair go?'

That was the sort of thing they could keep up forever, and they did keep it up for the rest of the week, Kevin being so animated and so friendly in his teasing that at last he had Moira smiling and Lin wondering what he was up to. It wasn't like Kev to go to so much trouble for nothing.

Willow Creek was too far away for a weekend, so they went to the local dance at Pike's Crossing on Saturday night. They picked up a couple of nice little birds there and had a wonderful night. It was just like old times.

From Thompsons' they went to Carrs'. There Kevin took to the cards again and played as if it was his life's work to lose money. He had had runs of bad luck before and lost money but never like this. It looked as if he wouldn't believe the cards. He would go the limit on two pairs and look as cool as a cucumber when somebody put down three tens. Lin lay on his bed and watched, depressed by Kevin's bad luck and awed by his mild indifferent expression. After three nights' play he borrowed fifty dollars from Lin against his cheque.

'I don't see it,' said Lin. 'What you get out of it. If you drink, you get something. You get your skinful anyhow.'

But the mystery filled him with respect and Kevin's self-control with admiration. He gave the money willingly, telling himself with pride that Kev never welshed on a debt. Though a funny fellow in some ways.

After they finished at Carrs' they went back to Willow Creek, Kevin sitting silent in the car, showing no emotion but seeming to fade a little. The marriage that was old talk to everyone else was new again to him.

That night Gloria tried to get into bed with him. He thrust her out furiously with his hands and feet so that she slid to the floor, and she got up and scuttled back to her own bed, but he knew he had made a mistake. She had seen the worst he could do and it wasn't bad enough. He could not deal a blow; his hands stayed still when they should strike out. She had his measure now.

Sure enough, she got nasty.

The incident had broken the silence. In the morning he opened his eyes when she was feeding the baby and instead of closing them again and shamming dead he said, 'Where's the money coming from?'

'What money?'

'That dress. The shoes. The bloody teddybear. Where are you getting the money?'

'Not from you, so mind your own business.'

'What about your bloody doctor's bill? I paid that, didn't I?'

'Too bad. It'd have all gone on the crown and anchor by now so you're no worse off.'

She sounded just like his aunt punishing the ears of his meek, defeated uncle.

'Where is it?'

'Where you won't find it. And I ain't going to tell you so don't wear yourself out asking.'

For an answer he seized the shabby white handbag she carried with her everywhere and shook its contents out onto his bed. Though the dismay in her face had made him hopeful, he founded only a dollar bill and a few cents — which he took just the same. It was not for the sake of the money.

He was too afraid to speak to her again. His only refuge was the dark cave of sleep, his only defence the glass wall of silence.

He kept up the search for the money, which was also a substitute for conversation. It had rules, like a game. He never looked behind her back and if she was in the room he always looked, even if he wasn't serious. As they lived, to turn a picture and run his fingers over the paper backing was as much as saying hello. When he had more time he searched seriously and she watched him without ever changing her expression. Once he thought, she wouldn't make a bad poker player, and that was the friendliest thought he ever had about her.

One night when he was drunk he came up from the bar and turned the whole room upside down without a word: emptied drawers onto the floor, dragged out suitcases and opened them, shook out her clothes and felt hems and pockets. The only time her face changed was when the baby woke and cried, and even then she didn't move but lay in bed looking at him. He came for the bed then and she slid out, throwing the pillow towards him as she went. Nothing there, nothing under the mattress. He gave it up and went away, trying to convert the disorder he was leaving behind him into a triumph.

Gloria began to clean up without too much distress. Oh, well, she said to herself in a tone she had learnt from her mother, while he's doing that he's not doing something worse. He must think though that she'd never heard of banks. There was a caché in the room where she kept her marriage certificate (for fear he made the baby illegitimate by tearing it up), her bankbook (because what he didn't know didn't hurt him), and any money she needed to have in cash, but she made sure that was as little as possible. The publican's wife would have minded her money if she had explained the situation but she didn't feel inclined to do that. Having the position of a married woman was all the pleasure she got out of life, except for the baby, and she didn't want to spoil it. When she started work full time as a housemaid she had said, 'Don't tell Kev,' hoping they would suppose he thought the work too much for her. Ha ha.

At Harriotts' where the shearers went next there was poker every night again. Kevin won at first and acted as if he would go on winning forever, playing high and annoying the others by forcing up the bets. Then he started to lose and lost even faster than he'd won, but with such a steady look on his face that it took a while to realise how silly his play was.

Though he didn't show any feeling, Lin got the idea that he didn't enjoy the game any more. It had got on top of him.

'Why don't you give it away, mate?' he asked one night as Kevin got into the bed next to his.

'I like it,' said Kevin, with a yawn intended to express indifference.

Lin thought, 'You don't play as if you liked it.' He watched Kevin come to the card table every night as if it was some sort of test.

'You must hate money, to throw it around like that.'

'Luck's got to change.'

It wasn't a matter of luck any more. If he did get a big run, it would only make more of a fool of him. Lin made up his mind to refuse to lend him money if he asked. To his way of thinking, that was what a good mate would do.

Kevin didn't ask Lin for money. Instead he tried to put an IOU into the centre. It was Jack who had raised the bet, and seeing the slip of paper he said quietly, like a priest interpreting a point of religious procedure, 'Take your stakes back. I'm putting my hand in.'

George who was standing behind him reported later with awe, 'A full house, he had. Three aces and two fours.' So the worth of his gesture was known. It imposed on the others then, and in a moment only the fallen cards, the last of Kevin's cash and the embarrassing slip of paper were left on the table.

As he gathered them in he said, 'You should let me chase my money,' covering himself with a show of anger.

'It takes money to chase money,' said Jack. To mend the situation, he added, 'You're staying over at Willow Creek for the weekend, aren't you? What about a game on Saturday night? You can have your revenge then.'

That was the end of the poker game. Kevin had so much feeling to hide that his face looked frozen when he came to lie on his bed and read a magazine.

'Wouldn't play with them if I was you,' Lin murmured, under the pretext of consoling him. Great hopes.

There wasn't a crown and anchor game at Willow Creek. On Friday night Kevin went down to the two-up school hoping to get back some of the money the unseen power owed him. He lost again. Though it wasn't his game and he had meant only to give it a flutter, the effort of getting away with the remains of his cheque was so great that he came away shaken, knowing for the first time what a hold gambling had on him.

It was only nine o'clock, which left a lot of the evening to fill in. He would have liked to spend it quietly, drinking a few cans with Lin in his room, for instance.

Lin must be in the bar with the rest of them. It would be a big night because the gang would start to break up tomorrow. As soon as he thought of that he knew he had better turn up there and look pleasant if he didn't want to lose face forever. His position with the gang was shaky enough as it was. He was puzzled and dejected at the change that had come over his life. That marriage — he took no account of it, yet ever since it had happened he found himself doing what he didn't want to do, as if, once you gave away one little bit of your freedom, you lost the lot.

At the noisy, crowded bar he stood next to George, who asked, 'Where are you heading for, Kev, now that the season's over?'

He didn't know. He hadn't thought about it. That meant he would drift back to Murrigong to Gloria's family — which didn't bear thinking of.

Why didn't he shoot through tonight, go to Queensland, change his name?

He couldn't be bothered.

His reckless fit was over. When he sat down to the poker game on Saturday night he was calm and careful, ready to get the best out of the cards. The hands he got weren't bad either, not wonderful but a lot better than he had been getting. The trouble was that, not having a big enough stake to start with, he couldn't afford to back a good hand when he got one. He let himself be bluffed out twice when he had the winning hand. Though he played as well as he knew how, kept his head cool and went slow on the beer, all he could do was lose as slowly as possible. By midnight he knew that his money wouldn't hold out and he would have to leave with his head down and his pockets inside out.

Not him. Not Kev Drinan. The beer he had been drinking had reached him by then, so that he looked with amusement at this prospect. It was time. Time for something.

The winning idea came suddenly and lit his face with a gentle smile.

He got up, saying, 'Deal me out this hand, will you?'

They thought he was going to the Gents', but he went up to the bedroom and switched on the light. That woke her up and she was out of bed in a flash when she saw where he was heading, but he got there first and picked it up. It came neatly out of the blankets wrapped in a cocoon of flannelette, but it was nasty to touch, wet and warm, soft and alive, like somebody's insides. It was harder to hold than a string bag, wobbling and sagging everywhere, but he got his hands under it and raised it over his head.

'Put the baby down, Kev,' she said in a full-toned whisper.

'Where's the money?'

She stared at him and her lips moved, but this time nothing came out. She wasn't so sharp now, not by a long way. Smiling at her, he began to take little steps backwards towards the balcony door. He thought it would be a nice touch to stagger a bit, but that was a mistake. Though he wasn't reeling drunk he wasn't sober enough to put it on and he almost went over.

'Come on. Where's the money?'

'Put the baby down,' she whispered as if she was making love to him. 'Put him on the bed. You can have the money.'

He shook his head and backed again.

'Put him down, Kev.' She was licking her lips now. She wouldn't make a poker player after all.

Without taking her eyes off him, she felt inside the cover of the mattress in the baby's crib and took out a plastic bag. He could see ten-dollar notes through the plastic. She threw it on the floor at his feet and said, 'That's all I've got. Put him down.' She might have had nothing at all. She had kept her last fortnight's wages in cash for the journey.

'Come and get it.' He raised it higher, grinning at her, thinking he'd get into bed with her when he came back. Might as well. Then it stiffened and squalled. He got tired of the game at once and lowered his arms. She was there and snatched it, and he picked up the money and went.

His luck really turned when he got back to the game, so that he could have cleaned them all out if he could have kept them playing but Lin came in with a girl about half-past one and the others made that an excuse to break up the game and get away. Lin and the girl were both at the giggling stage. Lin had a bottle of whisky and he wanted Kevin and the girl to come up to his room for a drink, but the girl saw through that, not being as far gone as she looked, so they sat down at the card table and drank the whisky out of beer glasses. After three sips, the girl said, 'Excuse me one moment,' in a modest tone that suggested she was off to the Ladies', went away and didn't come back. Kevin said, 'Ah, it's the oldest trick in the book,' but Lin thought she might have passed out somewhere, so they went to look for her and outside the smoky room the cool night air struck Kevin down. Lin got him to his feet and up the stairs.

'This has been one hell of a season,' he thought in dejection as he steadied Kevin down the corridor to the door of his room and went away to his own.

Far gone as he was when he fell on to his bed, Kevin must have noticed something, for his sleep was filled not with a dream but with a strange dreamlike atmosphere, as if the walls had come down and he was sleeping in his bed in the middle of a great plain.

When he woke up, she was gone. The crib, the teddybear, the blue plastic, the clothes, the baby — all gone. He felt the great stone slide off his shoulders, closed his eyes again and slept till late in the morning. Next time he woke, he thought it was a funny thing she had left just when he gave in. Well, who cared? That was his good luck. Wide awake now, he looked at his watch and wondered if Lin was ready for a hair of the dog. 'Better get dressed,' he thought, and then, 'Hell, I am dressed,' and started to laugh to himself, though the laughter nearly split his head open. Have to tell Lin that. He got up and washed his face in cold water, had a shave and went off to find Lin.

Lin was gone, luggage and all.

At Murrigong Lin pulled up outside the Thomases' house and the sound of the car brought Mrs Thomas out. She paid no attention to Lin and not much to Gloria, but put her arms out to take the baby, settled him in the crook of her arm and fixed her whole attention on him.

'Mum, I've left Kev.'

'Not much like you, Glor', is he? Got a bit of a look of Charlie.'

'Mum, I've left Kev, if you're listening. And you might say hello to Lin, who's driven me all the way from Willow Creek.'

He hadn't had much choice, thought Lin. He had had a terrible night, finding Gloria and all her gear in his bedroom, Gloria at the sight of him starting to howl and climbing up his arm like a monkey, begging him to take her home till he had to promise, to shut her up. He didn't know what it was about, either — only that Kev mustn't know. Just as well, because the way Kev was it would be hard to tell him anything. Four hours' sleep he had had on the sofa in the lounge and she had grudged him that. Now he had a headache, a bad taste in his mouth and a feeling that he'd been taken for a mug since he first laid eyes on Gloria. Not only by Gloria, either. Why did they all pick on him? Didn't they know he was Kevin's mate?

Used to be. Kev would be looking for a new mate now all right.

Lin had gone wrong somewhere right at the beginning, and things had never gone right since.

Mrs Thomas gave him a sour goodday and he returned it just as sourly. Gloria took no notice. She knew how he felt and she didn't give a damn.

'What about Dad, Mum? Will it be all right?'

'Never mind your father. I'll look after him. What's this rash he's got on his neck?'

Lin had the luggage unloaded, for the last time.

'You'll come in and have a cup of tea?' said Gloria.

'No thanks. I'll be on my way.'

He looked back before he got to the highroad. Mrs Thomas was still looking at the baby as if they were the only two people alive on earth, but Gloria gave him a wave, and, after all, he waved back.

Once a mug, always a mug.

A Bottle of Tears

♦

While Rita was waiting in the corridor outside the doctor's office the door opened and the doctor himself came out, shepherding a tall, thin man on whose face there was a look of intense concentration.

The doctor recognised her and said, rather irritably, 'Are you next? Go in,' so she went into the little room and stood looking aimlessly about at the desk, the examination couch, the lighted screen on which a chest x-ray was hanging, her mind quite occupied by the question of whether or not she should sit down, when the doctor came back and hurried across to the screen, exclaiming, 'It isn't yours!'

'I wasn't looking,' she answered, 'so it doesn't matter.'

He put his hand on the frame of the x-ray, meaning to remove it, but it drew his gaze again and he looked at it with pain and anger, muttering, 'I wouldn't want to see that in your chest, never,' unconsciously revealing his affection and giving her the impersonal joy one feels at the sight of a fragile-looking plant growing in conditions that bear witness to the toughness of the species. He was indiscreet, she perceived, because he was concentrating so much on the x-ray that he wasn't quite aware of her presence.

With an effort he put it away and, setting Rita's in its place, he produced a complete change of atmosphere, like an Elizabethan scene-shifter.

'Why don't you stop wasting my time?' he asked, pretending severity in order to subdue a smile of joy which would have been really excessive.

'As good as that?'

'Couldn't be much better.'

He opened a book and began to ask routine questions more seriously, and Rita gave the expected answers, but when their eyes met they both smiled, and as Rita was walking to the door her feet performed an irrepressible dance step. She looked back smiling at the doctor, who said, 'No silliness, now.'

'Everything in moderation, even silliness,' she answered, and closed the door behind her.

Outside the weather was splendid, with warm sunshine and a small wind playing in the street. A wonderful day for a walk, she thought, and set off to walk down Oxford Street to Foy's, meaning to drink a cup of coffee on the piazza and look at the park. On her way she paused outside the second-hand shop to smile over a framed panel of looking-glass decorated with a painted white swan, green reeds and a pink waterlily, and decided with surprise that it was pretty.

Suddenly, the money she had saved during months of austerity began to run in her veins and she went in to ask its price. Inside, on a table covered with dusty china ornaments, she found a narrow silver vase and bought that too. She promised to call for the panel and left, quite unrepentant, carrying the vase and planning the redecoration of her room: a dark floor — get rid of that dirty old carpet and polish the boards, she thought, drawing on her energy as freely as on her bank account — no whatnot, no epergne, no jokes except the glass panel, a Lalique swan on the mantel and a white rug with some pink and some green in it. She walked on, planning happily, without noticing her progress, until the laughter of children on the piazza reminded her that the schools were on holiday.

There were only half a dozen children after all, darting about and laughing with upward glances. Then she saw the bubbles, puffed out of a pipe masked with flowers high on the shop-front. The breeze was juggling them and letting them fall, and a little girl who had caught one opened her hand and looked into it with a painless cry of disappointment.

One bubble — how bright it was in the sunlight, outlined sharply with blue and purple — performed a slow descending dance and drifted past a young woman at one of the tables, who let it go and turned smiling to speak to her companion in a language Rita didn't recognise. This was a moment of poetry, a compound of the sunlight and the greenery that framed the woman's head, the foreign voice at home and at ease and the memory of an old map of the Terra Australis that had always prompted her imagination; and she thought, they are the real inhabitants, the migrants, the first since great-grandfather.

How did that thought bring Matt so close beside her that his absence was really a shock? Almost, she had turned to speak to him. It was one of those strange moments when one feels that a previous experience is repeating itself, but she had never been here with Matt. Of course, of course, the woman at the zoo.

Rita sat at the table drinking her coffee, seeing again the tall fair woman in the checked topcoat, standing at the top of a rise, looking down at the basinful of blue water flagged with white sails, saying 'Wunderschön' with quiet satisfaction. It was then that Matt had been standing beside her.

There is something about that trick of the mind, fusing past and present, that moves the heart extraordinarily. Is it oneself one greets with such sadness and astonishment? Rita drank her coffee thoughtfully, gazing at the park but after all without seeing it. Only the stream of traffic that flowed past the park, with the weaving of movement and the flashing of sunlight complicating its surface, drew her gaze and entered her thoughts. When she had drunk her coffee, she went inside to the telephone and rang Matt's office.

When he came to the phone, she said uncertainly, 'Matt? This is Rita.'

The silence that followed was just what she expected, for the underground river of malice ran so far beneath the surface in Matt that he could never be nasty at will; but she was frightened by it for all that, feeling that nothing she knew of Matt was of any value and that at the other end of the line there was an unknown, unlimited power to harm her.

'I don't see much point in this.' Matt was angry, but only Matt, after all.

'I changed my mind, that's all. You don't have to change yours on that account, of course,' she added in a false and arrogant tone that dismayed her. 'I just thought I'd tell you, that's all.' She waited, exposed to the abominable black receiver, feeling tired all at once, thinking that it would be a relief if the blow fell now. How easy it would be not to love at all!

'You really mean it?' Matt's voice was full of reverence, not for her nor for love, but for good luck, which he respected as other men respect money and fame. It was true that Fate was strict with him, and his wit, his kindness and his good looks were slightly tarnished by an amiable resignation.

'Is it all right?' With joy and relief, Rita began to laugh.

'Where are you?'

'I'm in town, at Foy's.'

'I can get the afternoon off.'

'I can't believe that. I'm sure this is just the day you have to work back.'

'No fooling, this is my day. Can you stay where you are? Half an hour, not much more anyhow.'

'All right. I can do some shopping and meet you on the terrace.' She was inclined to laugh at Matt, the scientist ruled by the stars (ruled by every bloody thing, kid; the stars and science, prenatal influences, economic laws, the boss and what have you), but there did seem to be some magic about the day which allowed her to repair so quickly that moment of loss and isolation.

Upstairs in the dress department she found a green and gold dress that seemed to be made for her, and when she tried it on she considered her reflection in the fitting-room glass, that reflection of a reflection one never sees otherwise, the profile of a stranger about to walk away, and was astonished as usual by its beauty.

She had been a plain girl and had become a beauty unexpectedly when she grew up, and the only thing in her face that she recognised as her own was the mark of her inward anxiety, which remained like the ghost of a frown when her face was in repose and gave her a gentle, sympathetic expression.

Today for the first time she could accept her good looks without uneasiness as an accidental glory like the weather and the new dress, having discovered transience as the flaw in everything that made it her own. Matt, too, she thought — remembering the urgency of his question, 'Can you stay where you are?' — wanting that one moment kept for him till he came; having just embarked on the current, she thought, of course I can't, and felt wise, experienced and full of courage.

But, as Matt was walking up the steps towards her, she felt quite deformed by nervousness, marooned in a nightmare on a stage to play a part she didn't know and feeling that everything she said to him from now on would be a desperate guess.

She looked at him for a cue, but he took her parcels in silence, looking happy but remote, and his happiness weighed her down with responsibility as if he had given her something fragile to carry.

'New dress,' she said as she handed over the big box. He grinned and took a slip of paper from his pocket, saying, 'Lottery ticket.' He was nervous too, and their laughter sounded forced.

They didn't talk much until they had closed the door of Matt's room behind them and begun to make love readily and without grace, like awkward swimmers getting into water where there is no danger. Rita said then, 'I had the experience of losing you suddenly. It was one of those moments, you know, that you seem to have lived through before, and I thought you were with me for a minute. It wasn't that I found I couldn't live without you, you see — it's so easy to begin to falsify things' —

'Is that what you're afraid of?'

'Oh, the things I'm afraid of,' she was shaking her head, 'they're too ridiculous to mention. Missing the train, losing the key, not understanding the directions, not hearing what the man says. You could overcome any one of them but there are too many.' Her face was bright and heavy with embarrassment, and Matt, quite startled, said, 'Nothing to be ashamed of.'

'What you're ashamed of is just the thing you are. You'll cover it up even with something worse.' She was silent for a moment, then she added, 'Gulliver tied down with threads.'

'What's that?'

'Gulliver tied down with threads, that's what I am.'

Matt didn't quite follow but he was glad to see her beauty restored.

'You know, Matt, I think I could change, perhaps, but I couldn't bear to have it expected of me.'

'I suppose I can stand you as you are.' He added, 'What you don't see is that happiness is pretty commonplace really. Anyone can have it, even people like you and me.'

This was said without irony and Rita could find no word for it except politeness, but it extended the meaning of the word.

'There's nothing new, is there? About being lovers, I mean. It's all in the past, like a graph that's been plotted already.'

'What was I trying to tell you?'

'And now I know.'

Matt said, 'Let's go out to dinner tonight. Somewhere really good, where we can dance. I'll ring up and book a table.'

'Somewhere with a view of the harbour. I could wear my new dress. You know, I never knew what those places were for, before.'

'Some people eat there regularly.'

'Very nice of them, too, to dress up and dance divinely and eat lobster thermidor on our account.'

'Probably they don't look at it like that.'

'Probably not.' Rita was smiling. She had always felt most alone in crowds and in public places, and now she was thinking that she would never really belong to a crowd again.

It was a wonderful evening, and in the elegant restaurant they did not seem out of place. 'Nothing went wrong,' Rita said when they were back in Matt's room, 'but if anything had, it wouldn't have mattered, and that will always be the main part of love for me. All the talk about what love is,' she added, yawning, very slightly drunk, 'I can tell you what it isn't. It isn't an abstraction. I love you has meaning, but the word love has no meaning; it's a participle, particle, something or other.'

'Grammar, for God's sake,' Matt said, laughing and putting his arms round her.

They fell asleep so close together that Matt woke up, hours later when the room was beginning to grow lighter in the dawn, because her sobs were shaking his chest like a grief of his own.

He whispered, 'Old girl, what's the matter?' But she shook her head and went on crying.

When she tried to speak, the man at the clinic appeared on the surface of the storm like flotsam and was drowned again.

'What man?'

He thought he heard the word 'dying', or was it the end of a sob followed by a brief sigh? No; she said coherently then, 'It's a man I saw at the clinic today, a man who's dying.'

For Christ's sake, he thought angrily, why bring that up now? He said, 'How do you know he was dying? Nobody would tell you a thing like that.' But he knew it in spite of himself, for the conviction that had been in the man's eyes and the doctor's voice was in Rita's crying too.

'An accident.' The word was cast up broken. She said again, 'An accident. I connected a face with an x-ray. Something the doctor said.'

There will always be someone dying somewhere, he thought, astonished at this simple device for destroying happiness, and his memory returned to him something it had kept intact, Rita saying in a queer, affected voice, 'I don't think I'm capable of happiness.' At the time he had shouted, 'What damned sickening nonsense,' but after all it was the queerness of truth, a deepsea fish hauled to the surface.

'If you'd seen his face —,' Rita sat up to look for a handkerchief, and in the twilight he saw a relationship of chin and shoulder that was like the first glimpse of the person one is going to love. Oh, well, he had promised to love her as she was, and now he knew what that meant.

'It seems terrible that I didn't think of him all day,' she said, still wiping away tears. 'It was such a wonderful day.'

'Your crying won't help him, kid.'

'No, I know. If I put my tears in a bottle and sent them to him, it would be nothing, a bottle of salt water. He'd look at it and wonder what the hell. What else is pity, anyhow? If I knew him, if I knew what to say to him better than anyone else, it would all be the same to him. Not because he's dying but for what he is now, cut off.' She took his hand, saying, 'Matt?'

'Yes, my darling?'

'I've been an absolute fool, haven't I?'

As he realised what she meant, his love extended to include the dying man, who was not, after all, an intruder.

Goodbye, Ady, Goodbye, Joe

♦

The low hill on which Joe's and Ady's old farmhouse stood lay in a loop of a little river, which had been growing bigger during three days of rain. In front of the house and a hundred yards below it, the banks were flat and covered with round stones, and there, the river had been spreading into a shallow lake with ripples visible at its advancing edge. Since the rain had stopped, shortly after noon, Joe had spent long periods at the kitchen window, watching. Where the river ran behind the hill, the banks were steep and the bed narrow; he knew the spot, out of sight five hundred yards away, where the water would spill over into the gully and run down to join the new lake, turning their hill into an island. This was the event that established the flood for him as a full-sized one with its modest place in history, so when the swimming water advanced round the side of the hill he called out to Ady with a note of satisfaction in his voice, 'It's through the gully, Ma. Here it comes.' Plenty of go in it still, he thought. He had had to wade through floodwater on his way back from seeing the cows onto high ground, and, feeling it clutch and drag at his high rubber boots, imperious and cold as death, he had been astonished at the force of it.

The old woman came shuffling to stand beside him at the window. 'Stay out of my garden, you devil,' she said angrily to the advancing streak of water. They stood then, staring while the new river ran down into the new lake, and Joe, who had lived for nearly seventy years on this farm at the centre of the world, thought of the two miles that separated them from their neighbours across the river, the eight miles between the farm and the town where their daughter Roslyn lived with her husband and children, the hundred and ninety miles of railway that connected the town with the remote, humming and glittering city of Sydney, and saw himself and Ady at the edge of all that distance — not at the world's centre, after all, but at its edge. He felt prompted to turn and speak to his wife, but idleness had made them shy with each other. They lived alone unless one of the grandchildren was spending a holiday at the farm, but they were always busy; now, with nothing to do, they were bashful, though full of goodwill, like young lovers.

'I'll put on a cup of tea,' said Ady, 'if you'll stay put to drink it.'

Joe grinned at the reproach. The flood attracted him constantly, so that he had left cups of tea standing to go cold and forgotten food on the table, to walk down the hill and gaze at the sheet of water welling towards them.

'Looking won't help,' she said. 'You ought to take your chance to get a good rest,' — as if the flood were a hostile neighbour against whom one must score what one could. She stoked the fire in the kitchen stove, lifted one of the stove lids and dragged the kettle over the circle of flames. 'It'll be in the town by this, I suppose.'

'Ros and Arnold never need to worry, living on the hill. Highest it ever came in the town was the window sills of the Commonwealth Bank, and that was the big one in 1920.'

Ady knew this as well as Joe, but, history being the man's province, she would have thought it unbecoming to mention it. She listened with respect while Joe talked, as he drank his tea, about the big 1920 flood and compared it with the flood of 1932, which they called their own, recalling, too, what he had been told about the flood of 1889. During the 1920 one, while they sat isolated in the farmhouse, the talk had been of the 1889, and of this talk Joe now told all that he remembered, Ady helping him with a question when he paused. Only the far-off, freakish deaths were passed over in silence. The calamities they recalled were small ones — 'Every plate in the cupboard broken.' These were offset by marvellous lucky escapes — 'But not a chip out of the cut glass in the sideboard. She picked it up and she put it down like a mother cat with its kittens.' What they liked best were the comic stories of survival, and Joe was telling one of them as he finished his second cup of tea. 'Rolled his clothes in a bundle, see, to swim it, and lost the bundle half way. So, no help for it, in he came, mother naked, and there stood the Reverend's wife. Come over to help with the cleaning up, and she stood there with the mop and the bucket like she was turned to stone. I don't think she ever got over it.' Blushing and grinning, he set down his cup and went across to the kitchen window, where his smile was extinguished.

'My word, she's moving, Mother. She'll be in your garden, all right.'

'Oh, the devil,' Ady wailed with temper. 'Oh, the dirty devil. My poor flowers.'

'Flowers are tougher than you think. My mother said the first thing through the mud after the '89 were the sweet peas. The old lady never forgot those sweet peas, standing up there pink and white with not a mark on them.'

'Don't mention mud to me,' said Ady.

'No use getting cranky with it, Mother,' he said, but, watching the water creep under the garden gate and wreathe around the gateposts, he thought it was easy to give it an evil character, and when it began to lick the walls of the small shed near the fence he nearly gave vent to an exclamation of temper, and only the thought of what he had just said to Ady made him suppress it.

They stood without moving and without noticing the passing of time, which the movement of the flood, in fact, replaced — the large, silent, reliable timekeeper that made clocks insignificant and the progress of daylight irrelevant. Joe thought of nothing while he stood there — watching was work enough — until Ady, in a thin, irritable voice, as if she were exasperated by a long argument, said, 'It's never been into the house.'

'There's always a first time. Reckon I might take up the carpet in the front room. Just in case.'

This was intended only as a formal recognition of outside events, however. He did not believe the water would come in, but he had begun to need a little insurance against it — like taking an umbrella to scare away the rain. 'You put a meal on, Ady, while I'm at it,' he said.

It was hard work pushing and lifting the old cedar furniture to free the carpet and then rolling the carpet up, but he worked off his nervous feeling doing it and took pleasure in the smell of eggs and bacon frying on the kitchen stove.

When Ady called him to eat, she did not mention the rising water until he started towards the window. Then she said, 'It's past the old high-water mark.'

'Only takes a minute to stop.' He sat down at the table and began to eat slowly and steadily. 'I'm going to curse myself for taking that carpet up. The old bookcase gets heavier every year, like a man's bones. I'll lay the carpet across the table here and put a couple of chairs under the ends.'

'It's moving so fast,' said Ady. 'I never knew it move so fast before.'

It had to be said sometime, of course, but Joe thought it could have been put off for a while yet. 'Always runs fast and runs away fast,' he said, choosing with composure the losing side of the argument. 'It's to do with the lie of the land. Not like the flat country, where it lies stinking for weeks.'

'Not as fast as this,' she said, stubborn and peevish.

'You be right and I'll be wrong,' he answered with belittling good humour, intending to annoy her. She should have held her tongue in the first place. Pushing his empty plate away, he said, 'Call me when the tea's made. I'll finish with the carpet.'

Before he had finished, Ady was at the door, saying, 'Joe . . .' in a timid voice. 'Joe, come and look at it.'

He would not hurry. He was pushing a chair under one end of the heavy roll of carpet and he finished what he was doing before he followed her to the back door, but, once there, he stared for a long time in the last of the daylight at the water sliding and caressing round the lowest step. There was plenty of go in it yet, that was certain, and the rain had come again as quietly as the dark.

'Could you manage a trip to the roof, Mother?' he said at last.

Immediately, Ady began to weep with childlike anguish. 'I'll die in my bed. Get on the roof as soon as you like. I'll die in my bed.'

'Now then, Mother,' Joe said, and reflected. Ady, with her arthritic hip, would scarcely be able to get out on the roof; with her bronchitis, she would not survive a night there in the rain.

'We'll bring the bed out of the spare bedroom and raise it on the table. You'll have to give me a hand. The rate she's coming, we'll have to move to keep our feet dry.'

It was such a relief to begin hurrying that they rushed at the bed and scrambled round it, pulling off the bedclothes and the mattress. They turned the bedstead on its side and tried to push it through the doorway into the hall, but they jammed it, blundering about like a couple of heavy old moths. Joe saw then that hurrying was a mistake, and he paused to get hold of himself.

'Better knock it to pieces. We're just wasting time,' he said.

'We had it out before. When we laid the linoleum. We took it straight back up the hall, feet first like.'

'So we did. Let me think now.'

For a moment, he stood leaning against the tilted bedstead jammed in the doorway, and what he thought was how quickly they had gone to pieces, wasting their strength in a stupid struggle with the heavy iron frame and letting darkness fall without lighting the lamp, as if they had already given in to the water and the night.

'We'll have a bit of light and start again.'

He made himself move steadily as he lit the pressure lamp. He would not forget again how easily panic started. To Ady, who stood watching him with scared eyes, he said, 'Keep the fire up, Mother. We'll be needing our cup of tea.'

Back in the hall, with the lamp set high on the hall stand, Joe talked to the bedstead as if it were a frightened horse. He was not going to admit anymore the existence of large, inanimate obstacles that reared up as if they had the devil in them. Somewhere in the situation there was a frightened horse to be soothed and talked into control. 'This way, now. Give her a little push, there, Mother. There you go, now.' The heavy frame slid into the hall and the difficulty of the removal was over, but the work had begun to tell on them. Ady stood ready to push, wearing a sour and fretful look that showed she was calling on the last of her strength.

'What about stopping for that cup of tea?' he asked.

'We'll just finish this first, if you don't mind. You and your cups of tea!' She gave the bedstead an angry push that did not budge it.

'Give it the rough side of your tongue; it might trot along and hop up on the table by itself.' He used the mean mildness of tone that always put her in a fury, and though in a way he was doing it for her, knowing her anger was all she had to drive her, it was a pleasure to him to be mean.

As soon as the bed was up on the table, Ady went down into the old leather chair in the kitchen. While Joe fetched the pressure lamp and put it on the mantelpiece, she sat there, staring at the boiling kettle as if she were trying to remember her connection with it. Joe had to make the tea, and when he took her a cup she accepted it as her right, like a bereaved person, saying only, 'You'd better open the door and take a look.' Even her weariness was nothing compared with her horror at the coming invasion of her house.

Joe was surprised that the water wasn't in already, they seemed to have been so long moving the bed, but when he looked at his watch he saw it was just on seven o'clock, so it had taken them only thirty-five minutes after all. He opened the door. Looking into the outside world was like looking into a pitch-dark curtained room. The timekeeper there had been moving as steadily as a clock. The water was brimming up to the doorway, and Joe wondered with sudden alarm what he was about, sitting drinking tea, with the mattress not on the bed yet. He had learned, however, how closely panic followed hurry.

'You make a thermos of tea and get something to eat ready to take up with us, and I'll bring the mattress out,' he said. 'Don't get your feet wet. I'll put my boots on. It it starts to come in, you leave everything and get up on a chair, and I'll finish.'

Though he told himself it was better to do a bit of wading than to get flustered, he couldn't help running for the bedding, and to disguise his urgency he put on a wild good humour, hurling up the mattress, saying, 'Heave ho, here she goes!' 'We'll be snug as bugs,' he said as he smoothed the blankets and stacked the pillows. Then he saw the first long, dark ribbon of water spring through the doorway and felt the sudden general weakness of fear.

'Come along. Up with you, Mother,' he said gaily. His feelings were in such confusion that when he climbed onto the table to lift her up he felt an irrelevant flash of high spirits, like a twenty-year-old on holiday. As he poured into a thermos flask the tea Ady had made, and put cake and biscuits into a basket, he experienced from time to time an extravagant delight at paddling about in the water on the kitchen floor, as if he were eight years old. He couldn't seem to keep hold of his mind, which went on bolting into childhood or the summer days of young manhood, and the water was over his instep, running cold and strong, when he handed the basket of supplies and a pocket torch up to Ady.

He put up the chairs, and on the seat of one of them he laid the hatchet from the woodbox, setting it down quietly so as not to draw her attention to it. If he climbed on a chair — Ady would have to steady it on the bed — he could knock a sheet of iron out of the roof, lift himself out, and somehow lift and drag her out, too. Otherwise, they were climbing into a hole with no way of escape.

As soon as he got up and settled himself beside her, he began to grin. 'Proper pair of fools we look, playing king of the castle,' he said.

She did not answer, because she was absorbed in looking at the water, and once Joe began to look there was no room for thought in his mind, either. It was sensational news, the water inching up the kitchen walls, disarranging household goods upon which a forgotten law had imposed places, making visible and extraordinary objects that custom had made invisible. Kindling tilted and began to float out of the woodbox; the boot-cleaning box shifted, swung sideways, and began to travel; the hearthrug grew sodden and sank out of sight.

'Cows'll be up to their bellies in this,' Joe grumbled. 'We won't be milking for months.'

Just then it occurred to him that cows were not the only perishable animals involved, that he might never milk again. The thought came as bold as a nightmare and stayed, altering his breathing and making his skin tighten on his body. He looked at Ady and saw that she had had the thought for some time already, and was sitting subdued and frowning, her mouth moving all the time as one lip worried the other. He wanted to warn her, saying, 'No, no, don't speak,' but it was too late for that.

'As if he had been the first to speak, Ady said, 'I never wanted to be left.' She would not look at him, and her uneasy, shifting glance as she watched the water gave her a look of insincerity. 'That was the thing I never liked the idea of, you going first and leaving me alone.'

Now it was said and there was no going back. Joe was so shocked that for a moment he could not think clearly. Trust Ady, trust Ady to open her mouth and say what ought never to be said.

'I always thought I'd have to go and live in town with Ros and Arnold. I never could live under the same roof with Arnold, or under any roof but my own.'

It seemed to him that she got some relief from talking, and he was filled with envious anger at first, but he soon travelled through the thought of her relief to the thought of her fear, and then to the knowledge that she, too, had to die. This knowledge offered him no escape from his solitude — poor Ady on her separate precipice was no company — but it brought on a black sadness that steadied him in his own fear.

'You wouldn't ever need to do that,' he said.

'You know what they'd be like — at you and at you to do it, and all the time thinking you were a nuisance. They'd be worrying about how it looked to other people — that Arnold especially, always worrying about how things look.'

It was dreadful to Joe that the prospect of death made no change in Ady. She thought of death, too, as a hostile neighbour against whom she must score small triumphs, and the expression on her face, superimposed on its look of trouble, was the ghost of an expression long familiar to him. That brought it home to him clearly that there would be no unknown resources in them to meet the moment. The people they were now must die. It horrified him, too, that he went on thinking about life, thinking new thoughts that were soon to be extinguished.

'It's bound to stop,' he said, with such authority that he

believed his own words; for a minute, his fear lay down like a dog. 'It's got a long way to go yet. Nothing to get in a panic about.'

Ady turned on him a look of morbid gentleness; it filled him with pity to see how fear had hold of her poor old sagging body. He ought to encourage her to talk, if it made her feel better. The trouble was that what seemed to help her was the very thing he couldn't stand — to have her soft, monotonous voice go on and on, not mentioning death but taking it for granted, not really facing it but thrusting the idea at him with sly, unconscious cruelty. For a moment, he looked at her, reflecting; then he swung off the bed and dropped down into the water.

'Where are you going?' she asked.

Without answering, he set out through calf-deep water towards the dining room. The current would have had him off his feet if he hadn't worked his way along the wall. Now the ruin and disorder of the furniture made him feel sick and angry; without looking round him, he worked his way to the corner cabinet, seized their two bottles of liquor and turned back.

The way back was difficult. The current running against him set him to a slow, wrenching dance that looked comic and made him sad. When he reached their fantastic temporary tower, he leaned against it with a feeling of affection, as if it were home and represented permanence and security. He handed up the bottles and paused a moment before he set off for the sink to fetch a bottle of drinking water and glasses. He had to control his movements so that Ady would not see how strong the current was. Hard as that was for him, as he came back holding the bottle and the glasses like a tightrope walker, concentrating on keeping his balance, he lived for a minute like a man in control of circumstances. It was a short release from the fear that had ceased to be terror and become a straining of the mind at a thought it could not hold.

'Here you are, Ma,' he said cheerfully. He handed up the bottle and the glasses, climbed onto the table and pulled off his boots.

'Ady was staring at the bottles with disappointment, as if she had been expecting something more like a miracle.

'Come on, have a drink. It'll warm you.'

The bottle of whisky was nearly full, and there was two-thirds of a bottle of the brandy Ady used for her Christmas cakes. The whisky was most likely to do the trick, he thought, and he poured some into a glass, added water and gave it to her.

Looking askance at the glass, she said, 'I can't drink that stuff,' and then turned to him with a shy, disturbed look that moved something in his memory.

'It'll do you good. Come on.' He poured himself a drink and waited for her.

'Nasty stuff.' She sipped and looked down into the glass with a sour grimace.

'Keep at it, now. You might get a real liking for it.'

'That would be a nice thing.'

At this, the absence of future pressed on them suddenly, the vast terminal brick wall of death reared in front of them and they gulped down the whisky. Then Joe poured them each a tumblerful and they gulped that, too — so open and shameful an action that each resented the presence of the other. In a moment, Joe put his hand over hers in remorse; her soft, shamed glance made him blush suddenly while it travelled in the dark lumber room of memory like a thin, hesitant beam of light. He poured her another drink and said, 'Come on, down with it,' sternly, to cover the shame of her willingness, and was all at once enveloped by a past day, as fresh as paint: cold sunlight and fine slippery grass growing on a steep bank like a wall behind them, Ady red and downcast as she straightened her dress, and himself saying miserably, 'After all, we're getting married Saturday,' and Ady — how astonishing it was, what a splendid present, to see that young face again — saying, 'It won't be the same now,' fretfully, so that he realised that what for him had been a sin against love was for her a domestic disaster in which her bridal finery had suffered. Being romantic, he had thought of love as a secret wonder Ady held in her keeping and feared that his lust, which had sprung on him like a lion, had done it a mortal injury — but Ady did not understand his bitter remorse or his need for comfort. His disappointment was deep, but he bore it with patience and put his arm round her tenderly. Since then the lion had grown old and died, become a disregarded old lion skin warm to the body in cold weather, but that mixture of tenderness and disappointment remained; it was the closest he had come to love.

Ady began to talk in a strange tone, irritable yet dreamy. 'I don't see why she had to change her name. That Arnold and his notions. I thought Rosaleen was a lovely name. Everyone used to say, "What a pretty name you've got, Rosaleen." I was set on her having a pretty name, mine being so plain. The first day she went to school, I remember, the teacher said to her, "Rosaleen. My, what a pretty name you have, Rosaleen." When she got home that day, I said to her, "Well, what did they tell you at school?" and that's what she told me — the teacher said, "My, what a pretty name you have, Rosaleen." '

'Kids always hate their names,' Joe said appeasingly, but he didn't really mind Ady's complaining, for he knew she was finding her way along the beaten path of grievance back to the past.

'I took a dislike to him the first day he set foot in this house. It wasn't my business and I held my tongue, but I never could like him. You're a cold fish, I thought to myself. You'll never let your heart rule your head. And so he's turned out. It was his job that took Rosaleen's fancy. She wanted to be the solicitor's wife and live in the town, that's the long and the short of it.'

'She's got her life, Mother, and she's happy enough in it.'

He wished he could find a door to the past again himself, for it was the only way left to go. He tried to summon up the face of the child Rosaleen, but the stout, cultured matron she had become obstructed his view. He thought again of young Ady, but her face, too, was gone; nothing was left of the picture but the tall bank and the tough, shining grass. The thought that the bank was still there struck him a strange, painless blow, a sensation that first he shrank from and then accepted. It grieved him to think of the grassy bank being drowned under the water, and that, too, was a remote and painless kind of grieving.

Suppose he said to Ady, 'Do you remember that Saturday before we were married?' He had a longing to meet her in the past, but it would frighten her, and she was absorbed, besides, in her lament, which was full of the same kind of comfortable sorrow as Joe's sadness for the grassy bank. Another drink would fix Ady, he thought and poured it for her.

He didn't have another himself, being rather uneasy at the odd thoughts that were drifting through his mind. When a man began fretting about grass being under the water . . . Then he looked at the flood as it rose, quiet and punctual, full of power, and felt in his smallness ashamed of supposing that it mattered whether he was drunk or sober. Something was required of him, some way of looking at the situation, but all he could feel was wonder that the water should be there, drowning the lounge suite and the kitchen clock. Because he found it difficult to believe what he saw, he looked round at Ady and found her lying asleep. Her withered eyelids, not weathered like the rest of her face, were as white as petals, her white hair lay loose about her face and she had clasped her false teeth to her bosom like a child's treasure. She was the link between reality and unreality. Now he believed it all.

The lamp on the mantelpiece went out and blackness invaded his eyes. He sat without stirring. The sound of the water was as quiet as a man's breathing, broken now and then by a gulping noise. He groped for the torch, disturbing Ady, who muttered angrily in her sleep, but when he found it and had his finger on the switch he paused. What good would that do? It was only for comfort that he wanted the light, and comfort was a sickly drink he had drunk enough of. Though his breathing was heavy and fear had a clenching hold on his intestines, he sat in the dark and tried to remember how high the water was. He studied the luminous face of his wristwatch. It was ten after ten — seven o'clock or nearly, just after dark, when the water first came in. Say two foot eight to the tabletop and two foot more to the wire mattress — she was past the tabletop all right. He would look in a minute. If he had thought of it before, he could have been calculating the rate of the flow. It would have done no good, but a man felt better when he could set himself to work. It gave him the feeling he was in control. That was a lie, too, but it kept a man upright on his feet. My God, he thought, seeing life from a new and shocking angle, that was a lie that walked with a man every day of his life.

He had chosen death for them when he went and got the liquor. He had not known it nor intended it; he had only, for a moment, stopped thinking about survival and begun to think of fear as the enemy. What a large, unexplored country lay inside a man — who would have thought he could be responsible for Ady's death? It was because he was an old man; a young man's grip on life was fierce, and he would grudge no suffering that kept him alive. Fear would have saved them if they had been able to endure it, would have given him the strength and the ruthlessness to drag and bully Ady out onto the roof, but he had put fear to sleep.

When he switched on the torch, the water had reached the wire mattress, and the sight of it turned him cold. He looked at his watch and saw it was a quarter to eleven. Then he thought, 'Why die?' It would be so easy, still, to climb onto a chair and escape to the roof. To lie down and die now seemed insane and disgusting, like a man's lying in filth when he could get up. He turned and seized Ady, shouted and shook her, but she did not stir. It was a long time before he could make himself believe that he could not lift her, and he did not stop trying until she uttered a pathetic long moan of protest. Then he lay panting, with his heart beating hard, and thought what he had to do. The thing he must not do was climb out on that roof alone. He groped for the whisky bottle and took a swallow of it where he lay; then he sat up and drank what was left. He found the brandy bottle beside him and sat waiting, thinking of nothing, till a moment of purpose arrived and he uncorked the bottle and began to drink. It was a small bottle and it was not full, but it took a surprising time to drink it out. He let the empty bottle drop into the water, but it stayed beside the bed and nudged his limp fingers like a hungry pet. He switched the torch on then, out of curiosity, and watched the bottle as it heaved and nuzzled among the trailing blankets, showing there was more movement in the water than showed on its surface, which looked like the shining black floor of the cavern of light. Joe looked at the water for a moment with idiot interest and then switched off the torch, because the light was keeping him awake.

The Army duck advanced steadily through mud and water, the soldier at the wheel frowning with concentration as he steered his course, his younger companion gazing about with a tourist's interest at the weird effects of the flood. It was early morning.

They had started out from their barracks to the town at midnight and after two hours' sleep had been called from their beds to begin rescue work. In the circumstances, they were inclined to exchange jokes and make cheerful conversation — though it had to be shouted above the noise of the duck's engine — since they did not wish to entertain the thought of what they might find. They were subdued, however, by the bearing of the passenger in the back seat, who sat upright, wearing already the awful dignity of bereavement, looking with calm authority at the devastation round him as if he owned a considerable share of it. He was a middle-aged man with pale, serious eyes, regular features too firmly padded under his rough, shining pink skin, and fair, tightly curling hair. The elder soldier thought of him as Curlylocks in spite of the sad circumstances. Both soldiers disliked him and were ashamed of their dislike, which deepened the unreasonable shame they felt at not being involved in the disaster. When they came in sight of the farmhouse and saw no sign of life there, they were full of remorse and pity.

'You stay there, sir,' the driver said quickly, with some tenderness in his tone, as he got down. He tried to walk with a confident bearing through the open door, but his tread was heavy.

Almost at once, he appeared again and said with a radiant grin, 'Come and have a look at this.'

Joe opened his eyes and reflected deeply. Someone close to him had said, 'Boy, what a party!' He turned his head slightly and saw the grinning face of a stranger, who said, 'Sleeping it off, Dad?'

He closed his eyes again to give privacy to his thoughts. Something quite astonishing had to be taken into account — what was it?

He was alive. If he was alive, Ady was alive, too. That thought brought a little warmth into his brain; he opened his eyes again and tried to lift his head but a fierce pain drove through it and pinned it to the pillow. Then he made sense of what the stranger had said. He was alive and he had a hangover. This time he rolled over and got up more carefully, bringing his head slowly erect — and, by God, there was Ady, sleeping like a baby, with her false teeth held against her chest like a rosebud. He realised then that he was holding the whisky bottle, which he must have found and clung to in his sleep. Looking down carefully, with respect for the condition of his head, he saw his son-in-law Arnold. The old leather chair was leaning drunkenly against the stove, with the upturned brandy bottle resting on its arm. Arnold looked at it with a mild, wondering look, but so intently Joe thought he was going to speak to it, and then Arnold looked round him. The soldiers were studying the high-water mark on the wall, and the elder one said to Joe, 'Only just kept your feet dry that time.' Quickly, with an apologetic smile directed at no one, Arnold hid the brandy bottle in the sink.

'As close as I want to go,' Joe agreed. He shook Ady by the shoulder. 'Hey, Mother, we've got company. Here's Arnold come to see us.'

He could swear she had her teeth in before her eyes were open. As soon as she was sitting up, he took off his socks, rolled up his trouser legs and, stepping down into the mud, made for the door.

There'll be plenty of damage done,' he thought nervously, trying to prepare himself, but 'damage' was only a word, and he was not ready for the physical shock that struck him through his eyes. He felt a great cry of outrage and protest rise in him, as if he were looking at the corpse of a friend.

'Six inches more and you wouldn't have known a thing about it,' the soldier said behind them, and he seemed to be far away.

How hideous the grey-black mud was, lying as heavy as flesh on the sagging fence. The small shed was lying on its side; slowly and with effort, Joe moved his eyes away from it. There was a great raw scar along the edge of the gully where the land was torn away, and tumbled across it there was an uprooted tree as ugly as a pulled tooth.

'Someone else would be cleaning up this mess,' he said. 'It's no job for an old man.'

He wished from his heart he had not awakened and need never wake again. It seemed to him that the instinct that made an old man turn away from life was the right one, but he was quickly ashamed of the bitter, complaining tone in his voice and of the despair that prompted it. He had not turned his head to speak to the soldier, and that was because he was concealing the look that he felt was set like a mask on his face — exactly that mild and wondering look he had seen on Arnold when Arnold saw the brandy bottle. Reality, with its unaccountable surprises, had always been too much for Arnold, and just now it was too much for Joe. Seeing this likeness between himself and his son-in-law, he felt a disagreeable small shock that woke him out of the great one. 'What were you expecting?' he said to himself angrily. 'You knew there was a flood, I suppose. Had long enough to think about it.'

As for Arnold, Joe knew from long experience, not needing to use words, what it was that Arnold longed for and had this morning allowed himself to expect — a moment entirely free from absurdity. In his mind's eye, Joe saw himself and Ady snoring on their wet, bedraggled, elevated bed, he with his bottle, Ady with her teeth, and slowly he began to smile. Some day he'd be dignified enough to suit Arnold, but, by Heaven, not yet.

He turned away from the door and went back to Ady.

'Come along, Mother,' he said, setting down a chair to make a step for her. 'You better start remembering how we move that bed back again.'

The Man with the Impediment

◆

As the undertaker's men lowered the old man's coffin into the ground, Minna crouched forward and spat on it. Seeing that it was Minna's last chance at the old man, Norman was not surprised, but the minister had to control a jerk of the head, and he turned towards her, converting an involuntary moan of protest into the cry, 'Miss Palmer!'

'Miss Palmer,' he went on sadly, 'have you no pity for your father, who may at this moment be facing the judgement of Heaven?'

Minna looked at Norman and asked him in a malicious, high-pitched tone, 'Have you no pity for your father, who may at this moment be facing the judgement of Heaven?'

Rebuked and defeated, the minister winced and was silent.

It was one of Minna's bad days, all right. The judgement of Heaven might not be so hard on the old man as the minister expected, seeing that a bad day for Minna had always been a good day for the old man, and the other way about: when he could be heard from the yard outside at his prayers — which consisted of shouting at God and demanding explanations — she would go about peacefully, cooking and minding the house, but if there was silence in the front room, she would begin to prowl and to mutter, working herself into a rage that came to a climax as she pushed the lunch-tray into Norman's hands, saying fiercely, 'You take it in. Go on, take it in. Don't you knock and leave it on the floor. You go in and show yourself.'

When he did go in, he would find the old man reading or writing, living a quiet, sensible life within the borders of madness, but later on the talking would begin in the front room and then rise to shouting and calling on God, and Minna would be calm again.

Now he said to Minna, 'Oh, come off it, Ma,' and the words came out quite clearly. His voice was like that; usually the words were a jumble no matter how he tried, and sometimes no sound came at all, but now and then his voice was let out of prison and he talked like anybody else.

He rarely called Minna Ma, and he did it this time especially for the minister, without knowing why — perhaps to shock him. That he spoke at all astonished the man and drew his troubled gaze; their eyes met but no communication was possible and the minister looked away, so joining all the others, the little boys who called out after him and ran away when he turned his head, the passers-by who gave him sidelong glances, the girl who had stood staring and yelping in the road when he tried to speak to her – that yelping was a noise that rang clear in his head after nine years. To this experience of the suddenly averted look he was accustomed, but not hardened.

He was suffering too much from his feet to worry much about the minister, since for the funeral Minna had got him to put on a pair of the old man's shoes. The laces tormented his instep and his big toe, straight and strong, thrust painfully against the leather that was forcing it close to the others. It would not do to take the shoes off in the cemetery, nor in the black car, either, but when they got out of the car in front of the funeral parlour he could stand the pain no longer, so he took them off and walked barefoot beside Minna to the hotel, where they had left the horse and sulky in the yard.

They attracted some glances — Minna more than Norman, for he, tall and silent, with his light-brown beard falling in broadening waves to his breastbone and meeting the curtain of hair that lay on his shoulders, was a familiar sight in the town, to which he rode once a month to go the bank. There was a branch of the bank at the store, but Minna would not use it for fear they were known to be rich and were accordingly murdered in their beds. She was afraid of the town, too, and scuttled along not only to keep pace with Norman's long step, but to hurry the moment when they would climb into the sulky and set out for the valley. Norman was not afraid; he had only a dislike of speaking, but it was easy to do their business at the bank without uttering a word. He would push Minna's cheque over the counter and wait in silence for the money, and nobody expected him to speak any longer — in fact, most people thought that he was dumb, and he was generally supposed to be an idiot, so that when the clerks at the bank had to tell him something about the account, they could never quite conceal their surprise at being understood.

The soles of his feet were so calloused that he felt like a shod animal, walking the pavement. When he had climbed into the sulky, gathered the reins and started the horse with a slap of them, he stretched his feet and braced them with relief against the rocking floorboard.

It was good to think of the old man put away, silenced forever, in the ground. He had a vague feeling for a different world that might come now, that he had been waiting for since he was small. But why then was Minna having a bad day? She made him uneasy, hunched there beside him with her lips shut tight, and staring at nothing. Probably it was from having to meet people; still, he could not help seeing her hatred of the old man as a full-grown wild beast that had lost its livelihood and would tear her to pieces. Suppose she moved into the front room and took the old man's place, shouting and arguing with God? He would be alone then, all right, for he knew how he stood with the rest of the world. She had begun to teach him that in his childhood by pushing him into the pantry and locking the door on him whenever a caller came — though he hadn't realised then what it meant; because Minna used to hug him when she left him and because in the pantry, into which sunlight seeped through a window submerged in the foliage of a Japanese bamboo, the atmosphere was mysterious but cheerful, he had supposed at first that it was a game in which some interesting visitor would come to find him. In the long run he had realised that it was no game, and the day came when he dodged Minna, ran through the back door and out to the front, where he watched from behind a tree.

That visitor had been an Assyrian hawker with a horse-drawn van; he had opened the back doors of it and there were dresses hanging up and rolls of bright stuff stacked on the floor — it was like a big cupboard on wheels. He had come out of his hiding-place, attracted by the cheerful look of the van's interior but more by the dark-eyed lively man holding up a blue dress, shaking out its skirt, rubbing the material between thumb and fingers and inviting Minna to do the same. Norman had come closer and closer and at last was standing beside Minna, who was so interested in the dresses that she didn't notice him. She bought the blue one and another, a white one with little red flowers all over it, and when the hawker said, 'What about a nice shirt for the little boy, Missus?', so that she looked up and saw him, she only smiled and bought him two shirts and a pair of pants.

She didn't try to hide him ever again. He knew she wanted him to hide and he felt mean, not doing what she wanted, but he was so interested in people in those days that he couldn't bear to. When Bert Evans the hired man used to come back from the store with the groceries, he brought the gossip of the district, too, and told it to Minna while she unpacked the carton.

'They was saying at the store that the Crouches are selling out — looks like the drought has finished them.' 'The Maclean girl is dead set on marrying the young fellow they got working there — she was in the store while I was there and after she left Mrs Breel was telling me her Ma and Pa aren't too pleased about it.'

Bert Evans was the only person they saw often. He had a wife who lived with him in the house near the old school that wasn't used any more, but she was in the hiding, dodging game more than anyone.

For all that, she had knocked on the back door one morning, had opened it without waiting and called out, white and staring, 'Miss Palmer, Miss Palmer, Bert's dead on the floor. Will you ring up the doctor, please?' Then she fell over. Her dress was buttoned up crooked and the pins were coming out of her hair. When Minna dragged her onto a chair and pushed her head down between her knees, the grey hair tumbled over her skirt and he saw the wrinkled nape of her neck. When she came to she started to moan and whimper.

'Get some fire under that kettle, Norman, and make her a cup of tea, while I ring the doctor.'

She had sounded quite different, as much unlike her usual self as Mrs Evans.

The next time he saw Mrs Evans, the woman who had

moaned and cried to Minna was tidied right away. Her hands were hidden in gloves, the nape of her neck under a knob of hair as smooth as iron, and her face and her voice were smooth and tight. She had come to say goodbye, and the tone she said it in seemed to prove that she could never possibly have moaned and cried at all.

Now that Bert was dead, it was Norman who went to the store. He set off the first time with his billycart rattling behind him as he ran along the valley road, eager to get to the place the stories came from.

Mrs Breel the storekeeper was a squarefaced, thickset woman with cropped grey hair and a permanent knowing smile drawn in wrinkles on her face. When Norman arrived, she was checking through an order for a farmer's wife.

'— and ten of sugar and a bag of flour,' — with a lift of her eyebrows she conveyed to the customer that someone of the highest interest had just come in — 'and we'll put it on the truck for you Tuesday. That's all, then?'

'Except the cheese and the onions. I'll take them with me.' She turned her head slowly to look at Norman. 'But no hurry, Mrs Breel. You serve the young man. I'm waiting for the papers anyhow.'

'Right, Mrs Willis. What can I do for you, young man?' Without giving him time to read his list, she added, 'Are you new hereabouts? I don't recollect seeing you before. A handsome young fellow like you, I'd be bound to remember.'

'Mr Evans used to come, but he died.'

'Then you're from the Palmer place, down the valley? That was real sad, about Bert Evans,' she said to the other woman. 'Not five minutes' warning, and he looked as strong as an ox. Not so old either, and he stooped down to tie his bootlace and he was gone. He was in here the week before, and I recollect saying to Mr Breel, it was a wonder a fine strong fellow like Bert Evans — ' With her face as smooth as a lake, she said to Norman, 'What's your name?'

'Norman.'

'Tell us what you want, Norman.' The skin round her eyes puckered as if there was some secret cause of laughter in his name.

'Six pounds of sugar, one pound of Red Label tea — '

'Doesn't he read well? Who taught you to read, eh?'

'Minna did.'

'Ah. Is that your mother?'

'Yes.'

'Who's your father, then?'

Staring at the floor, Norman searched his memory for some mention of his father, but found none. He was depressed, thinking he had spoilt the game with his ignorance.

'You should ask your mother.' Mrs Breel looked sidelong and merrily at the other woman. 'Now that's six of sugar, and one of tea, and what's next?'

It was mainly because of the laughter that Norman realised he shouldn't repeat this conversation at home. Laughter was out of place there. The store was in every way different from home — the openness, the bustle — he'd seen as many as seven people there at once just before the papers came in — and Mrs Breel's joking that made him the centre of attention.

'Well, well, here's the mystery man. Got any news for us today?'

He would shake his head and Mrs Breel would laugh.

One day a woman customer said, 'I think it's a shame to tease the boy, Mrs Breel. Everything isn't a fit subject for joking.'

'Why, it's between friends,' she answered gently. 'Normie doesn't take offence, do you, Normie? Here's a toffee for you.'

The toffee should be proof enough, surely. He accepted it with a serious look that showed he valued it mainly as a token of friendship, but the woman customer looked angry, and under her eye Mrs Breel began to look foolish and uneasy.

When he got home that day, he said to Minna, 'Ma, who's my father?'

All this time, under the face he knew, there had been another, sharp and wild and mean. She came for him and he dodged round the table away from her, but she caught him at the door to the hall. He was bigger than she was, but she was so wild that she pushed him along towards the front room where the old man was, pummelling with her fists between his shoulder-blades, screaming, but with faint little screams as if she was miles away, 'You ask him. You go in there and ask him. You get in there. Go on.'

He was seriously frightened when they came to the door behind which the old man was talking to God. Except for carrying in the tray on Minna's bad days, he had never had anything to do with the old man, and he thought of him as an awkward kind of domestic animal that Minna fed, and a noise that rose and fell like the muttering of branches against the wall. He stiffened and resisted her pushing; she fell and rolled on the floor, repeating still, 'Ask him!' but with a change of tone, as if she no longer wanted anything of Norman, but only to express her misery. He went to pick her up but she shuddered away from him when she saw him coming, crawled along on hands and knees to the stairs and pulled herself up by the newel, where she leaned whitefaced and closed her eyes.

The way was clear to the kitchen door. With his head lowered and his fists clenched he fled at full speed through the vegetable garden, across the paddock, along the river bank and into the bush, and slowed down only when he realised that the horror Minna shrank from was running with him. No use running. He did not really know then what his trouble was, but he knew from the beginning how deep it lay.

He sat down on a fallen log to get his breath. The ground here was buried under crisp dead leaves; he had seen a snake once, making an eddy and a rustle in the leaves before its tough, blunt head emerged. Though snakes need not be killed so far from the house, the sight of one, the first rustle in the leaves, the first stir of the grass turned him into an image of watchfulness with a stick in his hand and nothing in his mind but the thought of being ready to kill if it came to that. He stared at the leaves now, willing something to come, sitting so still that a bronze-coloured bird flew down and settled on the other end of the log, where it sank its beak into a cleft of the wood and began to clear it of insects. It was very important to him that the bird should stay; he sat so still it was like fading out of the world, breathing slowly and quietly until the bird pounced on the last insect, strutted, riffled its feathers and took flight. He felt much better because he had not frightened the bird away, and besides, he had a confused feeling that while he sat there, hardly breathing, he was giving Minna a rest from her troubles, too.

The sun was setting when he got back to the house, but the lamp was not lit in the darkening kitchen. The fire had gone out in the stove and Minna was not there. He lit the lamp and started the fire again. She did not come. He sat down to wait for her, but as the time passed he began to be frightened, thinking that if the old man got no dinner he would come looking for food. The thought of the old man's leaving his room appalled him — it was a ridiculous fear, for he came out to go to the out-house and even now and then to take a bath, and Norman had met him in the corridor; he was only a tall, stiff-jointed old man with a fixed, unseeing look on his face — but if he came looking for food and Minna wasn't there, Norman would have to speak to him, and he couldn't.

He fried two eggs, cut a crooked hunk of bread, put the food on the old man's tray and carried it to the front room, where he opened the door, put the tray on the floor, closed the door behind him — he wished he could lock it — and ran. What he had seen and heard was reassuring; the old man sitting at his desk with his back to the door and his Bible open under the lamp, reading aloud to himself in a hollow, complacent tone. He did not stop to take account of it, however, till he was back in the kitchen.

Minna did not come back that night. He fried eggs for himself and ate them on bread, going into the corridor now and then to listen in case the old man was complaining to God about his dinner. At last the lamp went out in the front room and there was silence. He locked up then, put out the lamp and went to bed.

When he came back from milking the next morning, he heard the door of the firebox clang against the stove, a sign that Minna was in the kitchen getting breakfast. His heart rose for joy, yet he felt shy about seeing her, and when he went in he could see by the way her glance sought shelter that she felt the same. They were sorry for the harm they did each other, but they could not say so.

The scene of the day before was never spoken of, but it left its mark. He gave up calling her Ma, from a feeling that family relationships were best not mentioned, while she was very quiet for a long time.

When next he went to the store, Mrs Breel greeted him with

her usual joke, and when he tried to answer he found that something had happened to his voice. It seemed to have taken fright; like a nervous animal it made a fleeting appearance, then shook off the burden of his words and darted back into his throat. Meanwhile above his stammering lips he looked with steady inquiry at Mrs Breel, trying to make some connection between her laughter and Minna's misery.

'Well,' — Mrs Breel drew herself up and assumed a formal store-keeping countenance — ' perhaps you'll tell us what you're wanting.'

Since things went no better when he tried to read the list, she took it from him at last and read it herself, wearing a look of self-righteous indignation as she filled the order.

There was no more joking at the store, and he missed that source of cheerfulness. From now on, the best part of his life was spent out-of-doors, fishing, watching and listening, sitting still to let the birds come near him. Whenever he did that he had a sense of fading into the background of the forest and recaptured the moment of peace that the bronze-coloured bird had given him.

He was nineteen when he met the tramp. Fishing in his favourite spot, he was sitting propped among the roots of a large tree, watching his line trail in the water, when he heard someone coming and looked up to see a very small man, with round prominent eyes in a childsized face, his forehead, nose and chin no bigger than the knuckles of a huge fist. He had a blanket roll over his shoulder; when Norman looked up he dropped it on the grass and squatted on his heels.

'You own this stretch?' His voice was thin but emphatic.

Norman wondered what his own voice would do; it crept out in a slinking way.

'Own the bank. Don't suppose anyone owns the fish.'

'Ah.' The stranger took his time deciphering this, reflecting on it and coming to his conclusion. 'Mind if I throw a line in, then?'

'Suit yourself.'

He watched the tramp thrust a hand into the roll of blanket and bring out a fishing line in a plastic bag, then he pushed across to him the tin of worms he was using for bait.

'Thanks, mate.' The tramp baited his hook, twirled his line and let it run through his fingers into the water. 'I was heading for Collingdale. Footing it. Must have missed the turning.'

'The left fork, you should have taken, this side of the store.'

'Thought I was getting nowhere, till I seen you. I followed the river, thought I was bound to get somewhere.'

'There's a track takes you to the main road, pretty overgrown now. I'll show you when you want to go.'

'That's fine.'

They sat resting after the effort of communicating, watching the lines drift in the stream.

'What do you do here, then? Mixed farming?'

'Did once. Not now. Few fowls, milk a cow. Grow a few vegetables, keep ourselves going. Not bad fishing in the river. Not biting today.'

He appeared to be whispering a series of secrets, but the tramp heard and understood.

'The Garden of Eden. That's what you've got here, mate. The Garden of Eden.'

'Got all we want. Have to go to the store for meat and so on, once a week, maybe twice.'

'You don't know your luck, mate. Who lives here, then, besides you?'

'Minna and the old man. The old man —' Norman placed his finger against his forehead in a gesture that seemed to him daring and sophisticated.

'Ah. Go your own way, interfere with nobody, nobody interferes with you.' He nodded in approval.

Norman pulled up his line. A fish had taken the bait and got away. He took a wriggling worm out of the tin, but instead of putting it on the hook, he held it writhing in his fingers six inches from the ground; meanwhile he closed his eyes and uttered a rhythmic run of sound, thin, lyrical and insistent, halfway between music and a human cry, repeated it, varied it and led it up to a harsher note on which he ended the call. He opened his eyes as a leggy, half-grown magpie alighted on the grass. It swivelled its head and faced its eye to the worm, advanced sidelong, teetering on its delicate claws, then came at a tiptoe high-heeled run and took the worm from the motionless fingers. It stood for a moment considering Norman as a donor of further worms, then stepped away and took flight.

'Getting real tame.'

He smiled affectionately, watching the bird's flight.

'Gawd, you're good with them birdcalls. They take long to learn?'

'Don't know. Been doing it most of my life, never stopped to count the time it took.'

'You've got the life, all right.' The tramp fixed a wistful look on his fishing-line. 'Shearing — that's what I would have liked. You got company, travelling with a gang. If you keep off the grog, you make your money in the season, the rest of the year's your own. You have to start young to be a shearer, or you never work up the pace, see.' He was too puny to be a shearer; it was a dream he was communicating. 'Been a rouseabout at a couple of sheds, seen them shear two hundred, two hundred and fifty a day. Ah. You don't have a pair of boots you can spare me, do you?' He raised his foot to show the sole of his boot, broken, with a piece of rag drifting through. 'Never make it to Collingdale like that.'

Norman thought it over. There were shoes to spare in the house; it was crammed with ownerless clothes — a cemetery, where clothes took the place of mortal remains.

'Nothing to fit you.'

'Too big wouldn't matter. That'd be fine. Pad them out with rag.'

Norman stood up.

'Come along with me.' He coiled up his line. 'I'll find you a pair. You better wait outside, though. Minna doesn't like to see people.'

'Who's Minna then? She your sister?'

'Mother, sister. Mother, sister. Same thing, I reckon.'

That thought he had never expressed, never even formulated before. It was a great relief to express it. At once he had thought, 'No use running,' now he surveyed what he had said and thought calmly, 'Well, there it is.'

The tramp was putting his fishing-line away in slow motion. He didn't look too well. His face grew paler and paler till it shone yellow and glossy like the surface of a can of cream.

Norman set off cheerfully, leading the way to the house.

'Find you a coat, too, if you want one,' he said, but when he turned, he found himself alone. The tramp was just visible among the trees, heading back towards the road.

'Hey!' he called. 'Hey!' making a great effort, and the cry sounded clear, but the tramp paid no attention, except to move away further through the trees.

That was the beginning of Norman's dumbness. It was not the loss of the power of speech, but the discovery of the use of silence. When he went next day to the store, he was still too intent on a feeling he could not put into words to be bothered with talking, so he put the list on the counter and waited to be served without speaking, and they served him without surprise and without comment. He realised what relief and what security there were in silence; those stammering greetings and strained answers were a tribute he owed to nobody and that, after all, nobody wanted.

The empty front room drew Minna, that was certain, but instead of moving in there to pray, she went in with a mop and a bucket and began to wash the floor. That was more like it, Norman thought, but the cleaning did not go on for long. Under the influence of some thought that kept her silent and abstracted and slowed all her movements, she left the mop standing in the bucket and began to go through the old man's desk. Spreading out old letters and documents, staring at them, folding them again, she sighed and went back to work but moved the mop idly, left it again and walked through the house, came back and said to Norman, 'I have to write to the lawyer.'

After that, she went back to work with more energy. When she called him in to move the table, she added, 'Who's to know who you are, if I die? You might be turned out of the house, even.'

At tea-time she said to him, 'There ought to be papers filled in when a person's born. There weren't any filled in for you.'

After tea, she got out pen, ink and paper and wrote the letter, while Norman watched with admiration. Her rapid easy handwriting was a relic of a different world, in which she had

had a horse of her own to ride, and a governess, and there had been four hired hands — a world that fascinated Norman, but was of no interest to Minna, so that he heard about it only by chance and in passing.

He took the letter up to the store and fetched the answer a week later from their mail-box at the side of the road. Minna tore it open and read it over and over, then put it on the table, stared at it like a gypsy reading the cards and fearing what she saw, and said, 'Somebody has to go to Sydney.'

'I don't mind.'

Poor Minna; worry made her shift her gaze from him to the letter, from the letter to the dim daylight at the window. Nobody else could be found to go to Sydney, after all.

'I'll give you a letter for the lawyer.'

It was clear that she thought Sydney a dangerous place, but he was not alarmed. He walked like a man in armour since he had learnt to do without speech.

My God, a guru.

As Jim Franklin walked through the waiting room past the bearded young man, he wondered why a guru would take to the law and what the old man would make of him. He was out of place there, but not laughable — he sat so quietly, with so calm a gaze, his bare feet were in such firm possession of their portion of carpet, that he almost made the office look ridiculous. Had he been corrupting the youth of the city? It was clear that he didn't give a damn if he had.

When his father came into his office ten minutes later, Jim saw on his face his reaction to the guru: a startled, irritable expression. Too disciplined to be flustered, he was nevertheless taken by surprise.

'I need you on this one, Jim. Did you see the young man outside?'

'He does take the eye rather, doesn't he?'

'Yes, indeed. Now, this is the Palmer estate, which is to be wound up, Arthur Palmer having died ten days ago. We had this letter first from Miss Minna Palmer — that's Arthur's daughter — with a query about the will, and I thought we should see her. Here's our answer, you see, and now this young man comes and brings this from her — preposterous, what can Miss Palmer be thinking of?'

'The bearer of this letter is the son of Arthur Palmer, born in the year —'

'Well, Arthur's wife was dead then, two years or more. One supposes that Miss Palmer is avoiding the word "illegitimate".'

'But wouldn't that dispose of his claim?'

'In this case, no. It's the grandfather's will — Alex Palmer was a very different man from Arthur. He had a reason and the reason is long dead and gone, and without issue, but there the will stands — all direct descendants, legitimate and illegitimate. You see what she says in the letter, that the boy's birth was never registered, and this is our only legal problem — though establishing identity will be a matter for some care. The human problem is that I cannot understand what the young man is saying. How she could have expected — perhaps she doesn't realise — I've asked him if his mother is alive, and if he would content himself with saying yes or no I suppose I could distinguish between the words, but he doesn't. You see the position. I am reluctant to write and tell her that I think the young man is incompetent. From what I can make out, he looks on her as his mother. She must have cared for him, perhaps since his birth. "Minna" is the only word I can make out.'

'A nice girl.'

'Oh, I think so.' Slightly reproving, Mr Franklin's tone indicated that Miss Palmer's niceness was irrelevant. Then he relented and stooped to gossip. 'I saw her only once, in my father's time. She was pleasant enough to look at, but unnaturally quiet. Very depressed, I think — the Palmers had declined from quite an aristocratic way of life, and Arthur's household was a sad one, I imagine. Arthur had very set ideas.'

'What sort of ideas?'

'Repressive, with the constant support of the Lord, you know. Divine authority for family tyranny.'

'The Lord must have withdrawn his support on one occasion at least.'

'Yes, so he must. Unless Arthur managed to justify himself to himself, you know, as such people do.'

'Was he mad?'

'Mmm. It's a moot point. A little extreme in his ideas, I think that's all. Well, now, it's a matter of getting into communication with the young man. I thought you'd be better at that than anyone else. Find somewhere for him to stay for a night or two, make sure he has funds, spend what time you can with him; try to explain to him that we need two witnesses, to register his birth. I'm afraid it's going to be an undertaking.'

'The first bit's easy. I'll take him down to Mother MacGonigal's, she'll give him a bed. For the rest, I'll do my best, I can do no more.'

'I'm sure I wish you well.'

'Mr Palmer,' said Jim, and was surprised, without reason, when the living statue turned its head. 'We think you should stay in the city for a day or two. Would that be convenient?'

He nodded.

'Do you have somewhere to stay?'

He shook his head.

'Would you like me to take you to a boarding house I know?'

He picked up the antiquated Gladstone bag from the floor beside him, stood up and prepared to follow.

Before Jim had walked two hundred yards with him, he was reflecting that most conversation was superfluous, undertaken for motives that were either fatuous or base. In the face of Norman's silence, he was ashamed of his own constant impulse to make conversation. On the other hand, he had to admit that he didn't like being seen with Norman, either. Norman attracted glances. Age sets in, thought Jim. I am a member of the bourgeoisie.

It was better walking through Hyde Park — that was like taking a stroll with a wild animal of a graceful and inoffensive species. Silence seemed proper; Jim was sorry when the sight of the Cathedral drew a word from him — what word, he didn't know, and the attempt to speak destroyed Norman's impressive calm. He did not try again; when they reached the boarding house in a street behind the Cathedral, he allowed himself to be handed over to Mrs MacGonigal in silence.

'Perhaps he talks better when he knows you,' Jim said to his father. 'After all, if he couldn't do better than that, no one would send him anywhere.'

'I take it you didn't get far with him.'

'He spoke once, when he saw the Cathedral, but I couldn't make out what he said. I must say he does rather well without. His command of dumbshow is impressive.

'That's all very well. He isn't going to tell us who his mother is in dumbshow, I suppose.'

'Mother Mac thinks he is meditating. Is he a religious gentleman, she wants to know. He does have rather the look. Got it from Arthur, maybe. Do you want me to spend the day on it tomorrow?'

'I know it's a great expense of time, but it's an old account, and I would like to get it settled.'

'I think I'll take him to the zoo. The hippopotamus might make him talk.'

The guru was waiting on the pavement outside the boarding house when Jim arrived. That was not consonant with the dignity of his calling, and besides, he was beaming, which gave him the look of a bashful hillbilly. He uttered a murmuring sound when Jim started the car, and later, when they were crossing the Bridge, he spoke a whole sentence which Jim kept in his mind, like a scholar studying an ancient inscription, while he considered possible topics and meanings: the weather, the bridge, the shipping, the traffic — horse! Horse and sulky! That was it — 'beats the old horse and sulky' — the guru was excited about riding in a motorcar.

'Not many sulkies about these days.'

While Norman didn't answer, he seemed to accept the remark as relevant. So far, so good.

At the zoo it became clear that the guru had a particular love of animals. The otters were trying to detain the young man who had been filling their tank with fresh water from a hose; one of them stood on its hind paws, rested its front paws on the rim of his high rubber boot and looked up at him in such a frenzy of love that he shook it off, embarrassed, muttering, 'Get away, you great sook.' Norman felt this deeply and watched with anxiety till the otters had forgotten their momentary grief and were sliding and diving into their tank again; then he smiled and moved on.

The smile inspired sympathy. Once he had hardened himself to the embarrassment of taking a six-foot bearded child to the zoo, Jim began to feel affection for him and was pleased with his astonished delight in the baby chimpanzees. One of these, seeing itself observed, lolled back in its swing, pulled chewing-gum out of its mouth in a fine thread and nibbled it back again while keeping its nonchalant gaze fixed on its admirer.

Norman said easily and clearly, 'Cheeky little beggar!' Jim felt as if one of the chimpanzees had spoken.

Things got better. It was as tiring as his first day in France but as in France he made progress. It had been right to bring him to the zoo, because there was a clear context to everything he said. Of the hippopotamus he said, 'He's an ugly one,' and he observed of the giraffes that they were tall, all right.

By lunchtime, Jim thought he was ready to attempt a conversation. In the restaurant, he chose a table by the window that overlooked the pelicans' pool, one with vacant tables on either side, and when the waitress had taken away their empty plates and had brought the coffee, he began, 'By the way, there's a difficulty about registering your birth. That's what we have to do now before we can go ahead.' He felt awkward; his eyes shifted and met the marble-white, strangely moulded pelican, motionless on a rock above the pool. Ever after, there was a dreadful sadness inherent in the pelican. 'In the case of an infant, you see, one needs the signature of a parent and a witness, the doctor or midwife, and as far as we know at present the procedure is the same for an adult. The question is: is your mother living?'

'Minna? She's living all right.'

'But I mean your natural mother. Miss Palmer, I take it, is your half-sister and your foster mother.'

'Mother and sister.'

There could be no mistake. The words came out as rough and plain as stones.

Out of the old documents the past event came sliding, alive

and venomous. I saw her once, his father had said — a sad household, somewhat lacking in balance. Somewhat, indeed.

'Well, that's not your fault, is it?' His voice sounded light and, shaken with shock, seemed to be shaking with laughter. He feared for a moment that he had given dreadful offence, but no — the look of the poor devil, the dawn of joyful astonishment deep in his eyes — as if Jim had brought him good news.

'Not my fault.' He nodded seriously. 'That's right.'

Jim was saying to himself, 'You're a lawyer. Do your bloody work and stop shaking.' He had to put real anger into the thought before he could control himself enough to get money out of his wallet and pick up the bill.

'Come on, then. Let's go and look at the lions.'

Looking down at the lions, Norman grinned with delight and began to talk, fluently but incomprehensibly.

Oh, hell. He wasn't making any effort now to be understood. He seemed to think that all difficulties were overcome. Where did they go from here? And how did Jim ever get into this? He gave up all attempts at swimming, let himself drown in the sea of babble. People were looking, damn it.

He touched Norman's elbow and drew him away, he hoped towards the gate. It wasn't just fatigue, either. There was a cold disgust in his gut that made him long for escape, though it shamed him. Norman went on babbling quietly as they walked. In front of one of the birdcages he stopped and fell silent. Watching a bird that was singing wholeheartedly, stating its claim perhaps to the lopped branch it was perched on, he stood as still as a tree, his face serene again. One could feel friendship for him, if only his situation did not demand so much pity that one shrank from the burden.

Unexpectedly, Norman pursed his lips and began to repeat the bird's song, softly at first, then clearly.

People had been eyeing Norman, of course, wherever they went, letting their gaze rest on the flowing hair and the beard, then flick downwards to the bare feet, but they had at least walked past with the air of keeping their opinions to themselves. Now that he had begun on the birdcall, he became one of the entertainments of the zoo. People smiled openly, children watched wide-eyed. It was strange how little this disturbed Norman. One could not even say that he ignored the spectators; he was like a wild animal that has not learnt the necessary, lifesaving fear of man.

And he was beautiful. Alien forever, but beautiful.

When Jim left him at last outside Mother MacGonigal's, he was determined to get justice for him and wished never to see him again.

He went back to the office and found his father.

'Dad, according to the Palmer will, how does an illegitimate son of Minna's stand?'

His father took the remark like a surfer taking a wave, then laughed and said, 'Don't find me any more Palmers, Jim, I implore you. I have my hands full with them.'

'No more Palmers, only Norman. That's the story — Minna's son, and Arthur's.

His father went white with shock, then red with rage.

'That poor girl. Oh, that poor girl.'

He had seen her, of course, in his youth. It took him a struggling moment to put his anger aside as irrelevant.

'Then the situation is completely changed. If Miss Palmer has a son, he takes the farm in fee.'

'In that case, the way is clear, isn't it? She registers his birth without stating the father's name, so the scandal is buried and Norman inherits.'

'One doesn't usually call that burying a scandal — I suppose it's a matter of degree.'

His father looked tired. Jim sympathised; he was exhausted, himself, from carrying the knowledge about with him.

'I don't think it's as clear as all that, you know. It's a delicate situation.'

'You mean that Norman has no right to exist.' The anger in his voice surprised himself. 'I agree. But he does exist, and she must want him to inherit.'

'Is he mentally competent, at least?'

'Oh yes. I think so.'

He was not so sure as he had been before he knew Norman's parentage.

'That fine estate — what a tragic situation. You are right, as far as I see it. Miss Palmer has to be willing to acknowledge him, it all depends on that. We don't, of course, know what her feelings are.'

'She sent him, didn't she?'

'There may still be difficulties. No doubt she will, if the situation is explained to her. You do your best to explain it to him, and we'll send her a letter.'

The junior clerk was sent to fetch Norman from the boarding house. He ushered him into Jim's office and left him there, grinning like a bashful lover.

'Well, sit down.' Smile and tone both forced heartiness. 'I'll try to explain the situation to you. We think we see a way out of your difficulty. According to your — to Mr Alex Palmer's will, the estate was to be divided, on the death of his last surviving child — that is, your father, Arthur —' He couldn't say it naturally, though he tried. And Norman's smile was fading. '— at Arthur Palmer's death, among the testator's descendants then living. If Miss Minna should have children, however, then the farm, which is of course the principal asset, vests in them absolutely.'

Damn it, I'm a solicitor. I'm doing my best for you. What do you want of me?

'So, you see, Miss Minna has to recognise you as her son and put her name on your birth certificate. There may be problems, but I'm sure they can be overcome. And there won't be any need to mention . . . the other business.'

He could not sustain Norman's gaze any longer. As he spoke the words, his eyes shifted. When he looked back, he saw the last of Norman's smile drain away, and he saw the hands coming up, but he did not realise the danger, because Norman had a gentle, puzzled look on his face and the hands seemed to be making an imploring gesture, but they went to his throat and tightened there.

He got his hand to the bell on his desk and pressed it. A long time after, he heard screaming that seemed to be far away, though it was the secretary screaming as she pulled at Norman's hands. The screaming brought his father and the clerks, who hung their weight on Norman's arms, till all at once he lost interest in the enterprise, dropped his hands and sat down, waiting quietly for the police and the doctors, who never let him go again.

Peppercorn Rental

♦

That Sunday morning Father had an argument with my younger sister Nell because Nell had brought home a baby parrot again. Nell wanted to rear a tame parrot and from time to time she appeared bearing a haggard fledgling which she fed and tended for a week and then usually neglected. Even if she didn't neglect them, they died, and Father had told her not to do it again, but here was Nell, looking rapt, remote and extremely dirty, carrying a tiny bird close to her chin and chewing a mouthful of rolled oats.

'Where did you get it?' Father asked. He was standing in front of the glass that hung on the back verandah, tying his tie and frowning at his reflection.

Frowning too with concentration Nell mumbled, 'Found it on the ground. Must have fallen out of the tree.' Very carefully she projected a small quantity of the moist and masticated rolled oats onto her lower lip and lifted the baby bird to nibble at it. She always said she found baby parrots lying under trees; she lied boldly and serenely and refused to accept improbability as evidence against her.

Father was confused for a moment, hesitated between justice to Nell and justice to parrots and said, 'Next time you find one on the ground you'd better leave it there.' The rolled oats disappeared while Nell whispered, 'Cruel!' Then she went on feeding the bird with insolent tenderness. Father recovered and reached the crux of the matter. 'If that bird dies, my girl, and I find out that you've neglected it, you'll be in real trouble.'

It was not like Father to miss the point even for a minute, but he was in his Sunday morning mood. Every Sunday we went to the homestead — so the whole family called my grandfather's house — for midday dinner, and every Sunday morning Father was absentminded, cut himself shaving and said, 'Oh Sunday morning!' like a curse, and made odd jokes which Mother seemed to understand but at which they never smiled.

Nell looked at him resentfully and said nothing. She was engaged at that time in a struggle with Father which I don't believe he ever noticed. If she was meditating an answer, Mother prevented it by coming in at that moment, discovering that Nell wasn't ready and hurrying her off to be washed and dressed. Eventually, she was ready before I was; I had just begun to write poetry then, and half an hour vanished between the polishing and the lacing of my shoes.

'She looks a different girl, doesn't she?' Mother said as Nell came out to the car, but really she looked exactly the same, for she still wore the remote expression which made changes like starch and polish, smooth hair and blue ribbon quite negligible.

She was still looking remote when we went to take our places at the long table in the dining room of the homestead, and I envied her. The conversation rose round me like the smell of dreary cooking, as it rises now when I think of it, though I can't remember a word that was said. The diary I was keeping at the time is no help; on Sunday evenings I used to make spiteful entries like, 'Dinner at Grandpa's. Nobody quoted Proust.' I see now that I was spiteful because I was frightened. Grandpa was a terrifying man , quite unapproachable because he found it as difficult to distinguish between human beings as between sheep. He could recognise qualities — strength, fineness of wool, intelligence and so on — and he did observe that some were younger than others and took the difference of the sexes into consideration quite as much as if people were sheep, but that was the limit of differentiation.

Grandpa sat at the head of the table carving mutton, the plates for the whole company of uncles, aunts and cousins piled in front of him, and now and then lifted his head to make a remark about the price of wool or the weather. The remark fell among the company and some adult felt it his duty to answer. That was not alarming; what frightened me was the dreadful game of musical chairs in which Grandpa's glance ranged the table and came to rest on one; having observed that this was a young one and a male, he would utter a suitable but quite unanswerable question like, 'What do they teach you at school, hey?' I should have liked to begin a singsong 'Five fives are twenty-five, fives sixes are thirty', but instead I used to blush and stammer, and for that I could never forgive Grandpa. 'That boy of yours is a fool, Molly,' he said sometimes. He knew pedigrees, as well as age and sex.

Dinner at Grandpa's was what is usually called a ritual, and one part of it really was one. As he carved the mutton, even to a slice for the Hugh Desmonds' baby, Aunt Lenore beside him dished out baked potato, baked pumpkin and beans until every plate but one was supplied. Then he handed down the last plate empty and carried the dishes over to the sideboard; when the empty plate came to Father's place he got up and served himself. Today while Grandpa was carving the mutton my cousin Ronnie, sitting next to Nell, shrieked suddenly, and Grandpa said to his daughter-in-law at the other end of the table, 'What's the matter with that boy of yours, Edna?' He didn't wait for an answer and the business proceeded quickly: Grandpa carved, Aunt Lenore dished out, plates were handed, Father stood up and Nell said clearly, 'Grandpa, why don't you ever cut the meat for Daddy?'

I would never have asked that question, but as soon as it was asked I knew that I was longing to hear the answer. I looked at my parents and realised how alike they looked. Though she was thin, dark and serious and he was stocky, pale and redheaded, with the urchin look men of that colouring still have in middle age, they met moments of crisis with an identical expression, this time of steady serenity which they seemed to maintain without effort. I had always taken it for granted that my parents loved each other — though the word 'love' was never spoken in our house, I think I measured their love for each other by their remoteness from us — and I knew, even, how love had announced itself to them as the subconscious stirring that makes the traveller gather his belongings together as his destination approaches. But I realised then that my parents were special people, and love not a common thing.

'Why, I reckon your father knows how to help himself,' said Grandpa and then burst out laughing. 'Knows how to help himself, I reckon,' he repeated and laughed louder still.

At this, a story that had been told to me in infinitesimal instalments throughout my life cohered at last. The word 'elopement', which had always been in the air around me, attached itself to my parents — and then there was Father greeting a blazing, whitish Sunday morning as 'good weather for running', the mysterious inferiority of our position, Mother's guilt and defiance when she talked about her rights — 'I've worked like a man on that property ever since I could ride' — and her warning, 'Walk straight up to your grandfather. It's the only way.'

Father wouldn't have been an acceptable suitor, of course, for in Grandpa's mind a man's relationship to his land was precisely the same as his relationship to his trousers, without which it is possible to be virtuous, but never respectable. As for women — I don't think his feelings about women had ever crystallised into contempt — they married men with land and provided its inheritors or they stayed home, like Aunt Lenore, and made themselves useful. But that strange two-headed monster, a couple in love, being outside his experience, had somehow defeated him. I didn't have to reconstruct the day because time had stopped there: in Grandpa's roar of laughter was his roar of rage, the wild chase across the paddocks and the high blood pressure that anguished female voices shouted to him to remember, and if every Sunday morning my parents renewed the day, the armour they had worn then was as good as new. This moment, strange and familiar, near and remote, was as exciting to me as that sudden change of focus in 'The Eve of St Agnes' — ... Aye, ages long ago, These lovers fled away into the storm' — and it excites me still, as if it kept something about love or time or poetry not yet revealed.

'Knows how to help himself,' Grandpa repeated and set off on a fresh burst of laughter as if the idea was a new one, but one couldn't grudge him all the enjoyment he could wring from a joke that had cost him several hundred acres and came his way only once or twice in twenty years. If Grandpa had known of my talent for poetry, he would certainly have blamed Father for it, but that would have been an injustice. I hope he never does discover where I got it, for with his blood pressure it might be the end of him.

The Trap

◆

In the nursery next door, the baby woke and wailed. Bill looked up smiling from his brief (Featherstone v. Constellation Candles and Domestic Wax). The desk on which the brief was spread stood at a window looking onto an overgrown garden. The ornamental peach which, more than the earnest estate agent, had sold the house to him, was in flower now. He faced it unseeing, absorbed by the sound.

It wasn't a cry of distress.

'Hold on, young Walt,' he said softly.

He had time to go to the kitchen, take out the bottle Ann had left in the refrigerator and set it to warm in hot water, while the crying grew louder and more demanding.

When he reached the side of the cot, the baby was rigid and frowning, about to bellow seriously; the frown dissolved to a fully extended smile and the crying gave way to clucking noises expressing joy.

'Just a big fuss about nothing, that was, wasn't it? Oh, yes. I know you. I see through you. And I bet you're wet. Yes, so you are. Now for the trial of strength and cunning.'

Changing the napkin was a game. He was sure the baby knew it was a game. The eye contact, strong as an umbilical cord, the squawking cries of joy as Bill tried to catch the rocketing heels, the giggle as he caught them and lifted them chookwise — five months old, but Walt understood more than anyone knew. As Bill lifted him clean and dry into his arms and carried him into the kitchen, he thought his heart might crack from love.

'No mother today,' he said. 'You're stuck with me and a bottle today. Your mother's in town, getting the hair done.' He faltered then, having let contempt filter into his voice when he spoke of Ann. I'll have to watch that, he thought, as the baby sucked without enthusiasm at the rubber teat.

'A very inferior drop,' he agreed, in compensation to Ann. 'Now, you can't be all day at it. Apply yourself. I have to get back to Featherstone and Constellation Candles. Do you know, son, they're putting up a silk against your father this time. That's a bit of a compliment, that is. But I think I have them. I think I see my way. Yes. Is that all you want, then? Well, don't wake up in an hour complaining that you're hungry, will you? OK, OK. Have it your way.' He held the baby against his shoulder, stroking the soft-boned vulnerable back till he evoked a belch. 'Great. We'll have a little stroll in the garden, then it's bed for you and work for me.'

Walking in the garden, he cradled Walt in his arms, knowing that he liked to watch the treetops, following the stirring of the leaves with a satisfaction Bill found calming. 'What I was thinking about Constellation Candles,' he murmured, as they followed the flagged path towards the old summerhouse, 'is this . . . what I have to establish, you see . . . ' He went on preparing his case till Walt checked him with a miniature adult yawn that made him laugh. 'I hope I do better with the judge.' He settled Walt's head against his shoulder. 'This garden is a mess, son. And I meant . . .' He had meant to make it into an Oriental vision of order and elegance. When he had followed the agent into the room, thinking, 'This will be my study', he had pictured a created landscape framed by his window. 'Well, I haven't been loafing. Bringing in the bread, that's what I've been doing.'

But things didn't turn out as one intended. No use saying that to Walt. He would find out for himself, and besides, he was asleep. He settled him in his cot, patted him on the cheek and went smiling back to his brief.

The smile was still on his mouth an hour later, but it vanished when he heard the front door open and shut. That was Ann, back from the hairdresser's. Now it would start. 'What do you think of it? Are you sure it isn't too long, too short, too tight, too loose?' (What I think of it is, it's a hairdo. Period. It's a bloody hairdo.)

This is a marriage like any other marriage, he said to himself firmly. Every marriage has its bad moments. He sat braced with a compliment, but Ann did not appear.

He spoke to his brief. 'We're in trouble, Mr Featherstone.' What would have been ten minutes' shame and irritation would continue now for days. 'Don't think it's real trouble. Not something wrong with young Walt.' He winced, regretting the thought for fear the gods were listening. 'Not even your troubles with Constellation Candles. No, it's the new hairdo. It's a failure. My mind's in drag. A hairdo!'

As depression settled on him, he admitted that Mr Featherstone's troubles were not involving, either. If Mr Featherstone's wife's great-grandfather hadn't started to make his candles in a moribund small factory on a stretch of land recently zoned for subdivision and now worth twenty-five million dollars, Bill would not be preparing to stand up in court and argue, with conviction, that the board of Constellation Candles and Domestic Wax was not acting in the interests of the company. 'Neither are you, Mr F.,' he muttered. 'Neither are you.'

An ambitious name, that: Constellation Candles. The man who had chosen it couldn't have foreseen that failure would bring fortune, war between parties, employment for Bill.

A shabby business, yet he liked it, enjoyed the contest, got satisfaction from his skill. It was not, however, what he had intended.

Staring at his brief, delaying the next step, he retraced the connection between Mr Featherstone's troubles with the Board and Ann's with her hairdresser. He had changed his course as a lawyer, got into Featherstone country, in order to finance a divorce. Twelve months after their wedding — as if twelve months was the proper period of mourning for a wedding — he had decided that he couldn't stand being married to ten fingernails, ten toenails, a pair of eyebrows that needed more attention than an indoor plant, and a body that, for all its beauty—

'Meat,' he muttered. 'Meat. Dead flesh.'

The old disgust was as strong as ever.

He had taken briefs at short notice, gone without sleep to prepare them, unhappiness driving him, and the hope of freedom.

Then Ann had told him she was pregnant. She had told him at the dinner table, after he had had a hard day in court.

'It does happen, you know,' she said, made uncertain by his astonishment.

But not, he had thought, to people like Ann. No reason why not. Frigidity wasn't a contraceptive, after all. She had still been taking modelling assignments, then; he felt that she lived in a world where pregnancy did not occur, or was terminated without delay.

He had said, 'It's . . . yes, I hadn't been thinking . . . It's a very big step.' He had got up, gone round the table and placed a Judas kiss on her cheek while he revised his timetable.

'The doctor said early May, the tenth, probably.'

He had burned with shame at this answer to his ugly, treacherous thought.

When he had first held Walt in his arms (that moment, unimaginable, indescribable, unforgettable) he had renounced divorce and sworn to make the best of his marriage, to give it his own best. And reminiscence, that beaten path into the past — he would give that up, too.

That was the pledge he was finding hard to keep.

No putting it off any longer. He got up and went into the bedroom. Ann was sitting at the dressing table, her head in her hands . . . no, her hair in her hands. She released it as she looked up at him, letting it spring outwards in two monstrous golden horns.

She said tightly, 'Look what he's done to me, will you? I'm a freak.'

She wasn't a freak. She was a goddess, and after even half a day's absence her beauty struck its blow again. He said, 'It's not as bad as all that. A bit unusual, perhaps.'

Why couldn't he tell her how this talk galled him?

Because this was Ann's essential self, so the blow might be mortal.

Because of his complicity. He had married a body; the punishment was precise.

It had been amusing at first, a world where a pimple was the onset of a mortal disease and a broken fingernail a drama which rallied one's friends. It had been like being backstage at the theatre. But he hadn't had marriage on his mind, then. Far from it.

'Unusual!' She faced her image in the glass. 'It's insane. Rinaldo's gone mad. Raving mad. Fame's gone to his head.'

He looked at her reflection, too, and sank into sadness. If only she was alive, passionate . . . he could stand the rest. Oh, she obliged. She made the body available at the expected time, only showing a little impatience if he spent too long on foreplay, trying to arouse her — a great waste of effort, that was.

'You might say, his fame has gone to your head.'

'Oh! Well, yes. You might say that, I suppose. If you weren't stuck with it yourself.'

'Can't you wash it out?'

'No, I can't. It's a perm. That means permanent. And that means I'm stuck with it.' She added in the same tone of sharp discontent, 'Have you fed him?' He forced his voice, hoping it didn't betray his feelings.

'Yes. He woke up a bit after two. He took about half the bottle. He wasn't keen about it, but he settled down all right. I left the bottle in the fridge — you can see for yourself.'

She nodded. The curls nodded expressively but he did not feel like laughing.

'I think I'd better go into chambers. There are one or two things I want to look up.' They could have waited till Monday but he could not. 'What time are these people coming?' 'These people' sounded unfriendly. He was sorry for that, but Ann had been so cagey about them — a distant cousin with the husband she hadn't met — that he didn't know how to refer to them. He was expecting Dave and Mabel, but he meant to make them welcome. She must surely know she could depend on him for so much.

'I said seven. That'll give me time to feed him and put him down before they get here.'

'If I'm home by half-past six, then?'

'Yes. That'll be all right.' She had picked up the hand mirror and was studying the permanent coiffure in profile. 'Honest to God, it's more like a hat than a hairdo.'

He left without answering, knowing she would not notice the omission.

In the car, he took the whole journey again, from that first moment at the chambers' Christmas party, when James had said, 'Look at that, will you, with Roberts! I wonder where he finds them.'

Roberts was a brilliant, ageing QC who betrayed a naive delight in the company of beautiful young women.

'I wonder what he's trying to prove.'

'It's quite clear what he's trying to prove. The wonder is that he thinks he's proving it.' The words were sharp, the tone indulgent. Roberts was loved for his generosity as much as he was admired for his brilliance. It was the girl who was set apart by the chatter.

Bill had looked and had thought perfection dull, preferring a more expressive face himself. The colouring was something, yes — true blonde, sea-blue eyes, complexion like the inside of a shell — Venus rising. She would do for a modish, elongated statue of Venus, if one cared for statues.

'It's harmless enough, a passion for beauty,' James had said, his tone showing a trace of it.

'Ah, but Roberts doesn't want us to think it's harmless, does he?'

On the other side of the room, she had turned her head to speak to Roberts. The voices round Bill had faded, his breath had stopped in his chest.

As he made his way discreetly from group to group approaching her, there had been in his excitement a warning of doom, but not of the particular doom that was waiting. Certainly not marriage. Damn it all, if she was with Roberts, he was entitled to suppose that she was raffish. Not marriage, but a great folly, out of a romantic French novel — asses' milk and emeralds — idealistic young barrister approaches grande cocotte . . . Well, he wasn't an idealistic young barrister any longer and, what's more, he had found out that he didn't care, preferred after all to do what he did best, and as for emeralds — emeralds for Ann, who washed plastic bags and pegged them next to her rubber gloves on a neat line above the sink! Even her extravagances were calculated and sparing. (Rinaldo would have no more of Mr Featherstone's money, that was certain.)

So he had reached her side. Roberts had drifted, as was his habit; she was standing alone.

He had said, 'What are you doing here? I wouldn't have thought this was your scene.'

'I come for the food.'

Her plate was empty. He had said, 'Let me be of service!'

He had taken her plate and brought it back with a cargo of sandwiches and savouries.

'It should be ambrosia. Food for goddesses.'

'I've never tasted that.'

She hadn't yet met his eyes. The answer had made her more mysterious. Either she was a moron who supposed that ambrosia was sold in David Jones' food hall or an introvert making a comment on her fate. Neither explanation had seemed to fit. He knew now that it was Ann's habit of minimal reaction: she told the truth because that required the least trouble. He hadn't known it then. There was so much he hadn't known then.

He had said, 'Will you have dinner with me some evening?' The eyes had turned to him, surveyed and, he had thought, accepted him. He had had trouble again with his breathing. Minimal reaction: as a social practice, it was remarkably successful, suitable for all companies, even the most enlightened. He knew now that it was not only the semblance of wit in it that made it attractive, but the indifference to others from which it sprang. Most people were impressed by indifference; few would wish to live with it. If he had got out at the first refusal . . .

He had wooed her with food. After the fourth expensive dinner, while they drank their coffee, he had suggested the weekend in the mountains.

She had said no.

'Don't think I don't like you.' She had looked at him with anxiety while he swallowed astonishment and mortification. 'It isn't that.'

'What is it then?'

She had found it difficult to answer, had shaken her head and shrugged.

'Morals?' Being angry, he had made an insult of the word.

'Oh no. No way. I don't disapprove of girls who do. Don't think that.' She had added, after reflection, 'I wouldn't have many friends if I did. It's the job I do, I suppose. The other girls you know — teachers, lawyers, people with university degrees — they're something in themselves, they can do what they like.' She had looked at him, troubled. 'You don't follow me?'

He had shaken his head.

'To most people I'm just a body, anyhow.'

'If you don't like the job, why do you do it?'

She had shrugged again. Discomfited, he had admitted to himself that that was the answer the question deserved.

'What do you intend to do, then?'

'Wait till somebody I like asks me to marry him.'

'Old-fashioned, aren't you?'

'Sex isn't?'

She was no fool. Meeting that hard, defensive intelligence, he was daunted.

He had looked to the waiter for the bill. Well, he had thought angrily, putting down his overloaded bankcard, he wouldn't be paying restaurant bills like this one again.

Up to that point, good clean misadventure.

Then had come the terrible month of nights spent in the tedious labour of recreating her face and her body, drawing them with detail on the dark. (Nowadays, to have sex with her, he had to think of other girls, other companionable times.) He should have endured, he should have held out. Passion dies at last, they say. This one would have been better dead.

He had gone back. Ann had been happy to see him. Of course

she had been entitled to treat him as a future husband, but he had still been looking for another outcome. He had had a fantasy: one fire lighting another — his own passion was so authentic, so unusual that he was sure she must respond to it at last.

He had been in the hands of an expert there, all right. Ann knew all there was to know about fending off the amorous male. That was the worst humiliation of many, being classified: the amorous male. Instead of the slow kindling of passion, the slow fading of happiness, then rejection. Her flatmates had answered the phone. 'Sorry. Ann isn't here just now. Can I give her a message?' 'Sorry, Ann just went out. I'm not sure when she'll be back.' They had ceased to recognise his voice. 'Would you like her to ring you back?' They knew how to deliver a message, those women.

Again he was tormented by images, in which she was no longer alone. Jealousy was an intolerable complication. There was only one way out. Now he had to plot, play the old friend, take the right tone, to make the approach to it. By the time he had said, 'Will you marry me?' (in the car, on the headland overlooking Caves Beach), they had had, not a relationship, but at least a shared history.

She had said, lightly and calmly, 'I thought you'd never ask.'

Again, an all-purpose phrase, which could have been taken as a declaration of love. He had chosen to take it so, at the time.

That summed up the whole marriage: not a relationship, a shared history.

He parked the car in his basement spot and ran up the stairs. He pushed wide the door of James's room and was so disappointed to find it empty that he halted, astonished at himself and uneasy. He wasn't in love with James, for God's sake.

This chewing over the past had to stop. Useless and depressing. He had forsworn it, many times. Work and Walt, that was what he had to live for. Work and Walt must be enough. But while he looked up precedents and took notes, he was pestered still by that uneasiness; it persisted like a physical symptom, mysterious, mild and threatening.

When he got back to the house, Ann was breastfeeding Walt in the dining room, wearing a loose wrapper over her underwear. He admitted to himself that the valkyrie hairdo did look odd; she looked as if she were getting ready to sing. She looked up with a smile and said, 'You're early.'

There was a good smell of coq au vin from the kitchen, the table was set with lace, glass and silver. Walt fell back gorged from her breast and grinned drunkenly at him while Ann dabbed at her leaking nipple with a cotton pad, stowed the breast away and fastened her brassiere. The semblance of happiness was perfect.

'Do you want me to take him?'

'Mm. Everything's just about done.'

'It looks good. Smells good, too. All the best for the long lost cousin, I see.'

'Just the usual.'

She had retreated. It was no use fishing for information about the visitors.

'I suppose I'd better get dressed.' She handed Walt into his arms. 'It wouldn't be so bad if I could dress to it, wear something lowcut. I could carry it off better.'

The hairdo. She had been thinking of that bloody hairdo ever since he had left.

He carried the boy away in silence. As he settled him down for the night, he thought, 'Don't fall for beauty, son. It's a cold, sour religion.'

He sat beside the cot in the dark until he heard the doorbell announce the visitors.

When Ann brought them in, he did think at first, 'Yes, Dave and Mabel.' The cousin was short and stout, with eyes like currants in a face like an unbaked bun. Beauty was a cold, sour religion, but there it was — he was a worshipper. He did not wish Ann less beautiful in exchange for any increase in warmth. The husband was tall and thin, his face marked by too much mildness and the idiot glint of rimless spectacles.

'This is Bill,' said Ann. 'My cousin Bridie. Bridie . . .?'

'Bridie McLeod. And here's the McLeod. Gavin.'

Gavin shook hands.

A pause.

Bill seated the visitors and poured drinks to cover the moment of awkwardness he couldn't understand.

Silence again. Each woman waited for the other to speak.

'Well, Annie.'

Unexpectedly, Ann smiled.'Well, Bridie.'

'I expect you got a shock when I surfaced.'

'I didn't even know you were in Sydney.'

'Came looking for work. Three years ago, now. I had a job with the Shire. Dad created when I left it, but shorthand and typing weren't for me. I thought I'd try Domestic Science, got a job in the laboratory while I was waiting for Tech to start. It suited me and I suited, so I stayed. Then Gavin came to work there, and there we are still.'

Bill asked, 'Why didn't you get in touch before?'

'I didn't know where you were. Doreen wrote to tell Mum about the baby and Mum wrote back for your address. And I tell you, Annie, I don't leave without a look at that baby or I won't dare to go home.'

'We just put him down. He's due for a feed at ten.'

'We'll wait him out.'

Bill began to find her likeable.

'How are all the family? And Colin? He must be quite grown up now.'

'Eighteen. He's helping Dad on the farm, never looked to do anything else. That was a real disappointment to Mum. She wanted him to get some training but she couldn't keep him at school past sixteen. With Dad backing him, of course.'

Ann, it seemed, was exhausted by that social effort. She retreated to the dining table, where she was making small adjustments to the setting.

Bill said, 'Your mother isn't in favour of farming?'

'It's a hard life, dairy farming, seven days a week. Mum says it's slavery. Dad says it's better to be a slave to your own land. You can't argue with them. Annie says you're in the law?'

'That's a hard life, too.'

'Your clients don't come bellowing to be milked at five in the morning.'

'You mustn't talk to a lawyer about milking his clients.'

'Bellow after they're milked,' said Ann, who seemed, after all, to have picked up something of Bridie's tone.

'I have known grateful clients,' said Bill, wearing a look of wounded dignity. 'And science is your line?' He placed the question between Bridie and the silent husband.

'Not mine. Gavin's. I weigh out the rats' food and clean the cages. He does the learned experiments.' She fixed Bill with a firm gaze and said, 'No, he doesn't.'

Gavin groaned. 'Bridie!'

'Doesn't what?'

'Torture rats. Cut them open. Infect them with nasty diseases.'

'The thought did not cross my mind.'

'Liar!' she said with a grin.

'Bridie!'

'He's safe. I can tell by his eye.'

'Well, I'll come clean. Just for a moment there, I did wonder.'

'I work in psychology. The worst I do for a rat is give it a head-ache, or a sense of inferiority. Of course, that may be morally reprehensible, too.'

'Is it all right if I serve up now? We won't have shoptalk at the table please. Not if it's rats.'

'Can I help, Annie?'

Ann called from the kitchen, 'No thanks. Everything's under control.'

'I suppose,' said Gavin, as they took their places at the table, 'that the Law has its moral dilemmas, too.'

'More than most, perhaps. Wine for everyone?'

'Thank you. Why more than most? I should think Science bears the heaviest responsibility. I think my branch, the study of human behaviour, is on the side of the angels — '

'Except for the mental sufferings of rats.'

'I believe,' said Gavin, as Ann set a casserole on the table, 'that Ann has banned the subject of rats.'

Bill laughed. 'I think you may have missed your profession.'

The conversation promised well and performed well, on the moral dilemma of nuclear scientists, pure knowledge against public good, the problems of barristers —

'Suppose,' said Gavin, 'by sheer forensic skill you secured

the acquittal of a murderer, who later committed another murder . . .'

'Oh, it's a paper case,' Bill objected. 'There isn't enough forensic skill on earth to defeat real evidence.'

'But you must sometimes secure an acquittal when your client is guilty?'

'Not to my knowledge. Not to my certain knowledge. Presumed innocent. Presumed innocent. That's the law and I serve the law.'

'But sometimes wearing your white hat and sometimes wearing your black hat,' said Ann.

That brought laughter and 'Good for you, Annie!' from Bridie.

Over the second bottle of wine, Bill asked, 'When did Annie become Ann?'

'At the model agency. Anny was a very big name in Paris at the time. Phoebe didn't think it was my style. She didn't think I could live up to it. Funny, you wouldn't think of Annie as a name you couldn't live up to.'

'That would set you back. Bridget. How would I go as Bridget?'

Gavin said, 'You stay as you are.'

'But would I be different?'

'That's a point. Does a change of name affect the wearer? Bill, having been disconcerted by Ann's answer, had begun to regret the question. Had there been a shade of malice in it? He was glad to make the topic general. Bridie studied him. 'You can be William as soon as you like.'

'Now what does that mean?'

Gavin said, 'You had better ask Ann. She has had the experience.'

They looked at Ann, who shrugged. She had not taken a second glass of wine and was not sharing in the high spirits of the others.

'It was part of a whole package at the time, make-up and clothes and so on. I suppose it must affect you. And then, there wasn't anyone around who knew me as Annie. I suppose that made a difference.' She added, 'I wouldn't like it if Bridie called me Ann.'

Something in this speech had affected Bridie, so that she ate in silence for some time.

Later, she was observed to be staring at Ann's hairdo.

'Well,' said Ann, 'what do you think of it?'

Gavin shone with pride. 'Be careful. She cannot tell a lie.'

Being full of innocent joy at the quality he loved best in Bridie, he did not notice fleeting expressions on the faces of the others.

Ann said, 'It looks like a giant's moustache.'

'But it's all right. It takes the eye but it's all right. It wouldn't do for everyone but it suits you. I can see it on the cover of *Vogue*.'

'It's more likely to be seen at the Baby Health Centre and in the supermarket.'

'Yes. I see what you mean.'

'I never did make the cover of *Vogue*. A toilet paper ad was my top.'

Bill preferred to forget the toilet paper ad. He wished she hadn't mentioned it.

Bridie said, 'A lovely picture, though. Gran has it cut out and stuck up on her wall.'

Ann was startled, then confused. After a pause, she said, 'A picture of Bob Hawke is a picture of the prime minister. A picture of me is a nice piece of wallpaper.'

'I didn't know you had political ambitions.'

As soon as he heard the remark coming out so smoothly in his own voice, Bill was ashamed of it. It had cut Ann so that she flinched. The anger he had swallowed earlier in the day was rising with the wine.

'Oh, come!' Gavin spoke severely. 'It's a valid point.'

And so it was. The comment had been not only sour but stupid.

'Well, it isn't a piece of wallpaper to Gran. It's a picture of you.'

Ann was at a loss again. Luckily Gavin was still pursuing the point. 'But to people who don't know Ann, that is so. I don't think the example is extreme. Her face could be as well known as the prime minister's but as a face without identity.' He turned to Ann. 'Does this trouble you?'

She looked back at him, cool and defensive. 'Not enough to put me off my food.' Bridie giggled.

'How did you get into modelling, Annie?'

'Oh, Uncle! Uncle paid the fees at the school. Uncle did wayout things out of sheer innocence, I think.'

'Like the evening dress.'

Ann blinked in shock. Bridie looked distressed, regretting her words.

'What's this about an evening dress?' Bill took care with his voice; friendly interest was the tone.

Bridie said at length, 'All the girls got an evening dress for the high school farewell. It was your first evening dress and a pretty big night. Aunt Alice wouldn't get one for Annie. Lousy old bitch. So Uncle Clyde sent away for one from the mail order catalogue.'

Weary and exasperated, as if they had been discussing the evening dress at great length, Ann said, 'I didn't want a dress. Clare was going to lend me hers.'

She stood up and began to collect plates.

'Mum said at the time, it wasn't so much for you as against Alice. There'd been trouble coming there for a long time.'

'I didn't want to be the one to bring it on.'

She left for the kitchen.

Bill would have liked to ask Bridie what this was about, but, shamed already by his attack on Ann, he did not like to show that he didn't know. Damn it, he should know. Was this altogether his fault? Since it was necessary to change the subject, it became difficult to think of anything to say. He got up to pour the dessert wine.

'Lucky we're not driving,' said Bridie with cheerful resignation. 'This is a lovely house.'

'That is not a non sequitur,' said Gavin, 'whatever you may think. We do not have a car. We do not have a car until we have a house.'

'You should see my mortgage.' Bill spoke with some pride, as if his mortgage were an expensive pet. 'Do you intend to build?'

'I'd like an old house, like this,' said Bridie.

Over dessert they talked about housing. There was no spirit now in the conversation; it faltered into silence. Over coffee,

Bridie said, 'Annie, I'll come clean. I've got a message for you. They want you to come back.'

Ann sat rigid, staring at something invisible.

'Gran says she won't die happy till she's seen you again.'

Concern moved Ann slightly. 'Auntie Em? Is she ill?'

Bridie grinned. 'Not she. Mum says she'll see her out. She's just made up her mind that she's on the wing. She does have a bit of arthritis and it's slowed her up. Mum says she doesn't have enough to occupy her mind. She's always been a worker, and now all she's got to do is walk around the paddocks and sit in a corner of the kitchen brewing up mischief. Mum's words.'

'That doesn't sound like Auntie Em.'

'No, poor old thing. Mum puts up with it pretty well, because she's always been such a good old thing and how do we know what we'll be like when we're old? Mum says, how do I know what you'll be putting up with from me? None of that from you, I said. Not for a minute. Into the Old Folks' Home with you. And Col says to me, you pack for her, I'll drive the car.'

'Your father was most upset.'

'Yes, Dad took exception.' Bridie laughed in astonishment. 'He thought we meant it. But Annie, wanting to see you, Mum says that's the only sensible thing she's done yet.'

Bill, already exiled among ghostly personages, was enveloped now by a cold wind of sadness. Ann, too, was an exile, a rigid and melancholy figure. Bridie became serious.

'The trouble is with Gran Caroline's stuff. You remember that big cabinet in the front room, with all Gran Caroline's china and silver, and that horrible big blue and gold affair with the picture on the front?'

Gavin said, 'The Sèvres vase. The family treasure.'

'The family curse,' said Bridie. 'Well, that's still there, but Gran's giving all the stuff away. Any second cousin that drops in for a cup of tea goes off with a cup and saucer. Of course Elaine found out and made a fuss. She felt it was her duty to write to Alice and warn her . . . poor Mum! They don't bully Gran about it, they bully Mum. It's that vase they're after. Elaine was so sure of it that she roped Alice in, never thinking Alice would lay claim to it. But Alice says that it was given to Gran in trust for her.' Bridie shook her head in despair. 'Mum gets a letter from Alice: "Will you please remind Emily of the agreement . . ." As if you could remind Gran of anything.'

'Bill is lost,' said Gavin. The kindness was intended for Ann. 'It is necessary to follow all these complications with close attention.'

'Gran Caroline was a Pom,' Bridie explained. 'A very high-class Pom. She came out here with the Governor's wife, as a friend, more than a paid companion. They were close. And Great-grandfather was a dasher, too; he owned half the valley and he built the big house when they married and all this stuff was shipped out from England.'

'Not the vase,' said Ann. 'That was a wedding present, wasn't it, from the Governor's wife?'

'Yes. The Vice-Regal couple, as Elaine puts it. Oh, Lor'. There's Elaine saying, as the widow of the eldest child and only son . . .' Bridie sagged under the weight of her own words. 'And all Mum can get out of Gran is, "Wrongs should be righted". As soon as she sees Elaine's car in the road, Gran takes off and leaves it to Mum.'

'You're not making this very inviting to Ann,' said Gavin.

'Mum says, the funny thing is that Gran's got all that stuff because Gran Caroline couldn't stand Elaine. Gave it all to Gran when she married so that Elaine wouldn't get her hands on it.'

Bill said, 'Your mother doesn't lay claim to the vase?'

'If it was Mum's it would go straight to the Saint Vincent de Paul. Dad's idea is to shear it in halves and give them half each.'

'The judgement of Solomon,' said Bill and achieved some acknowledgement from Gavin.

'If you came, Annie, you'd be sure of a cup and saucer.'

'She wasn't my great-grandmother,' said Ann sharply.

'Oh, Annie! Don't you start!'

Ann roused herself to say brightly, 'I wouldn't mind one of those marvellous pos. Do you remember them?'

'They're still out in the barn. If that's what you fancy.'

'The black one with the waterlilies?'

'Yes, that's there. I fancy the pansy pattern myself. No fooling, Annie. It would mean everything to Gran if you came back. It'd be a help to Mum, too, if it settled Gran down. We're going up for the long weekend and I said I'd try to bring you.

We haven't said anything to the old lady about it, she doesn't even know we got your address. We don't want to build up her hopes. But if you could see your way . . .' Bridie looked at her seriously; Ann looked seriously back. There was an area of silence here that neither would invade. 'Think it over, love. Gran's not the only one it would mean a lot to. Well, I suppose we'd better clean this lot up.'

'Don't worry. I'll stack it in the dishwasher.'

'Listen to that. I live to say those words.' Though her words were cheerful, she looked at Ann with sober concern, then at Bill with complicity.

'She takes it for granted,' thought Bill, 'that I know what this is about. I dare not ask; she would be shocked that I don't know.'

So was he shocked.

The evening was dead. Ann got up heavily, as tired from listening as Bridie was from talking. They stacked the plates and cleared the table in silence. Bridie said, 'Can I tell them you'll think about it?' Ann shook her head as if she were shaking off the request. Bridie sank hers as if she acquiesced in the refusal.

Mysteriously, it was a moment of sympathy and intimacy.

Walt woke and cried out. Everyone smiled in relief.

'I'll bring him out,' said Ann.

Bridie turned to Bill, saying, 'I hope I haven't upset her. I had to ask, you know.'

He nodded, bewildered, a stranger in his own living room. Ann came back holding Walt, bright-eyed, looking with curiosity at the visitors.

'Oh, the little love!' Bridie coaxed him into her arms, laughed as he rooted at her breast and handed him back, saying, 'No joy there, love!'

She was still subdued by disappointment.

'We'd better be off, Annie. Leave you to it. If you do change your mind about the weekend, let me know.'

Ann bent to kiss her cheek, deprecating offence.

Bill saw them to the door, saying a polite goodbye over what seemed to be the ruin of the evening.

On the way to the bus stop, Gavin fished for information.

'She's a handsome piece of wallpaper, your cousin.'

Bridie wished for a moment that he could have used a different bait — but well, that was Gavin.

'She always was a stunner. The love child.'

'The love child?'

She explained, 'When I was about ten — I suppose Annie would have been sixteen — I heard Mrs Addison say to Mum, "That Annie is going to be a real beauty, isn't she? It's generally the way with love children." At which I got the idea that married people had beautiful children if they loved one another enough. I wanted to look like Annie more than anything in the world, so I kept my eye on Mum and Dad hoping they would come up to scratch. Not getting much satisfaction, as you can imagine. Then there was the row about the evening dress, and the things that wretched woman said about Annie! I found out then what a love child was, all right. An ordinary bastard. What a comedown! I gave up wanting to look like Annie then. The price was a bit high.'

'I thought it was a mistake to mention the evening dress.'

'Yes. I know.' Bridie sighed. 'It was on my mind, I think, knowing I had to ask . . . bringing it all back. She was upset, poor Annie. No wonder, either. If you'd heard what that bitch Alice said. She called Annie a whore, like mother like daughter . . .'

'Charming.'

They had reached the bus stop. They were alone there.

'Nothing to what she said about Uncle Clyde . . . Uncle Clyde and Annie . . . oh, she's a proper bitch, is Alice.'

'She said that they had sexual relations? Because he bought Ann a dress?'

'Don't put it like that! It sounds so awful!'

'It is awful.'

'Yes. Well, it's going to be a disappointment to Gran. You'll bear me out that I tried.'

'Don't give up yet. I think he might talk her into it.'

Bridie paused. 'Did you like him?'

'Up to a point. I enjoyed his company.'

'If he talked her into it, it would need to be for a good reason.'

Gavin put out his hand and stroked her solid white neck. 'Everyone can't be as lucky as we are.'

'I wish Annie could be.'

They stood in silence, holding hands, until the bus came.

Bill woke in the dark, sober and depressed, and lay still, waiting in dread for enlightenment. The bad moment came back, as sharp as reality. He heard his own voice, smooth and spiteful: 'I didn't know you had political ambitions.' Smooth and spiteful and utterly bloody stupid. He winced at the memory of Bridie's face closing, of contempt in the flash of Gavin's glasses. A man who sneered at his wife in public was a social pariah.

From the next bed he heard Ann's peaceful breathing. She was sleeping the sleep of the innocent; her innocence didn't make him like her any better. 'They don't know,' he said to himself, aggrieved.

There was no excuse for him. It was a piece of intolerable behaviour. He could not swear either that it would not happen again. He hadn't meant it to happen last night. 'I am over my head in this,' he thought, and identified the vague misery that had haunted him all afternoon: he was in the grip of a passion again, taking the first steps on the treadmill. Lust, jealousy, hate. He hated her.

What was he to do?

He could make an improvement in his present situation by getting up and emptying his bladder; any relief would be helpful.

He got up carefully, not wanting her to stir, went barefoot to the kitchen door, switched on the back light and walked along cool tiles to the outside lavatory. The night air on his face defined his headache; standing before the bowl, watching the stream flow, he thought, 'This is what comes of living with someone you hate. Deterioration.' It would have to be divorce, after all.

And leave Walt? No!

'Look, you can't answer. You've shown that. You can't answer. You wouldn't be offering Walt much, sneering and sniping, bringing him up in a house full of hate. If you care for him, you'll let him go.'

What was he doing, standing there, staring down a lavatory bowl? Symbolic. He pulled the chain and wished that too was symbolic.

At least the action had broken his trance and set him moving. He couldn't go back to bed; he began to prowl the garden, glad of small discomforts, cobbles unkind to his bare feet, the night air cold, penetrating his thin pyjamas.

Divorce. Client country. The country, face it, of failure. How easy life had been till now. As all the way, maybe an A minus or a B plus now and then — being dropped from First Grade in cricket had been the worst of it. No penalty like having to give up Walt.

Divorce would cost him plenty — not only Walt, not only money, but social approval. Nobody would understand him. His mother loved Ann, all the more because she had at first disapproved in silence. 'Such a practical girl, dear,' she had said. 'Such a good little housewife. The last thing I was expecting, I must admit.' He couldn't explain to his mother that Ann's meticulous housekeeping was part of her devotion to the surface of things, that one was forever walking through a splendid façade into nothingness.

An ugly fact surfaced: some of last night's anger had come from the steady beam of love that Bridie had directed at Ann. He had wanted to destroy that.

This was squalor. None of it Ann's doing. This wasn't marriage to Ann. It was a worse and deeper marriage with himself. What she had said — 'A picture of me is a nice piece of wallpaper' — she hadn't been a façade then; that was the first time she had ever seemed conscious of her limitations. He should have welcomed that instead of striking out.

How happy was she? He saw her pinched, mortified face again. She hadn't retaliated, hadn't even apparently felt resentment. Perhaps she was the victim of passion, too. Perhaps her passion for respectability had stranded her in hostile territory. That was their first piece of common ground.

Divorce might not be his decision. He could name two barristers who would be happy to see the marriage founder; tired as he was, the thought of either of them as Walt's stepfather spurred him even to the most painful thought: Ann had been a different person last night — a real person emerging in that steady warmth, which he had never provided.

But she'd been cagey. She'd been cagey all right, hiding that family. He had asked and been fobbed off. But he had accepted too easily; he hadn't sufficiently wanted to know. That was lust. Lust didn't want to know. Flesh and a mystery, that's what lust was after. It was supposed to be a comic passion but it was no joke; it was a weary hunt through rough bush after a half-seen animal, ending in a desert where it left you alone.

He was cold now and tired from his perambulation from the back door along the stone path to the summerhouse and back again. He had made himself sufficiently uncomfortable; he went quietly into the living room, turned on the light and poured himself a whisky, feeling he had come back to the normal world. However, he had brought the truth with him. None of this was Ann's doing. She was guilty only of being Ann, and that was a fundamental human right.

A man didn't have to be ruled by his passions. He must change. That thought, which was frightening, brought back the dark. He needed something, a God, a guru; change was a small death.

He wasn't a child. He had some intelligence, some experience. Never mind about bogey thoughts. If you can't change yourself, you can change the situation. Look at it like this: two people trapped in a railway carriage on a lifetime journey. Never mind what brought them there. They were fellow-travellers, must know and accept each other.

Knowledge was what he was lacking. He could cure that, find out about this family problem, for a start.

It wasn't altogether his fault. He had tried. Bridie's phone call had caused Ann such astonishment, followed by an evening of abstracted silence, that his curiosity had been roused. He had even persisted. 'Just a distant cousin. I didn't know she was in the city.' 'You're not very keen?' She hadn't given an answer, had looked as if she were searching her mind for one. He had taken the easy solution, that Bridie and her husband would be a social embarrassment. That made him wince again. It was he who had proved to be the social embarrassment.

He hadn't known then what questions to ask. He knew that now and he would ask them. It would be an effort; silence had become a habit hard to break. He must keep the alternative in mind. He repeated the names of the two hopeful barristers and managed a smile. Trust the old Adam, he thought; he took his empty glass to the kitchen and went back to bed.

When he woke again, Ann was up and dressed, standing at the dressing table giving her face its morning scrutiny. She had plucked a hair from one eyebrow and was inspecting the other.

He said, 'That was a distant cousin? She didn't seem very distant to me.'

'I was just going to wake you. He slept till a quarter to seven. I've just put him down.'

He picked up his watch from the bedside table. Half-past seven.

'Why did you say it was a distant cousin?'

Ann was brushing her hair, tackling the great curls with energy. She answered briskly, without feeling, 'That's the other family. I'm not really her cousin at all, I suppose. My grandfather was married twice. This Gran Caroline was his first wife. That's Bridie's great-grandmother. His second wife was my grandmother. They say Gran Caroline, Gran Mary. You really had better get up. I'll start breakfast.'

At dinner he said, 'Tell me more about your family. You were saying, your grandfather was married twice.'

No doubt about it, she stiffened slightly.

'What's the matter with you? Skeletons in the closet?'

'I suppose you might say that. It was a scandal. Grandfather was old, Richard and Em were married, Alice was the only one at home. Gran wasn't much older than Alice. An old man's darling. She worked behind the counter in the local store. Look, what's the point of digging up the past?'

'I was put in a very awkward position last night. It seems to me that there were things I should have known that I didn't know. Bridie took it for granted I knew your family history.'

Ann nodded. 'History,' she said with finality.

'You're the one keeping it alive, it seems to me. After all, that's two generations past! Whatever dirt they did your grandmother! And this old woman who won't die happy till she's seen you, she must be very sorry for it.'

'Auntie Em?' Ann looked at him bewildered. 'Auntie Em's

never done any harm in her life. She's got nothing to be sorry for.'

Bill began to think he had missed the groundwork in a difficult exam subject.

'Would you mind telling me who all these people are? Alice, Em, Elaine . . . begin at the beginning.'

'I can't, can I? I wasn't there.'

'Ann! Proceed!'

He began to laugh in a kind of comic despair and got a smile from her.

'I wish you'd eat your dinner.'

'I'll eat while you talk.'

'I don't know why it's so interesting. Well, the first family, Gran Caroline's children are Richard, (he's dead), Emily (that's Bridie's Gran) and Alice; then Gran Caroline died and Grandpa made this scandalous marriage with Gran Mary. I can remember the way they used to call her Gran Mary. It was a kind of a put-down.'

'Families do that kind of thing very well.'

'Do they ever!'

Strangers on a train. It wasn't working badly. Some communication was taking place and Ann was showing a new energy, making fun of his manner, proving a tough subject for cross-examination.

He said firmly, 'Now to the second family.'

'Two daughters.' Ann paused, reluctant. 'Nora and Grace. My mother was Nora. She died young and Aunt Alice took me in.' She said defensively, 'I've told you all this. I told you I was an orphan and I lived with my aunt. She's the one in Queensland. She went to live with Doreen. You know about all that.'

There were, however, things he did not know.

'I can't tell you anything about my father because I don't know anything. Nobody told me. So that's that.'

End of story. Ann had retreated into a reserve in which she seemed to be contemplating a private source of tenderness. He did not wish to intrude. If only she ever turned that look on Walt . . .

The reserve persisted through the evening. At breakfast she was still contemplative.

He thought, she'll tell me more when she's ready. He was seeing her truly for the first time.

At dinner that evening, she said, 'Bill!' and paused.

Here it came.

'I did tell you, didn't I, that I'm illegitimate?'

'No.' He stopped to arrange his voice. 'No. Your own business entirely, but orphan is what you said.'

Ann said, 'Well, it's the same thing really, I suppose,' as if the matter were hardly worth consideration.

He was shocked at his own reaction. It wasn't her business. Walt's ancestry. Barnyard drop, riverbank special. Worse in the country. Squalid. 'Nobody thinks anything of it, these days,' he said and tried to carry conviction.

But if he had known, he wouldn't have married her. He was astonished to discover this about himself. He had taken his liberal opinions so much for granted. If he had known this, he would have dragged himself away.

'Who is your father then?'

She shook her head. 'I'm a real case. Father unknown. Mother a name in the family Bible.' The mention of the family Bible was comforting. 'Nora Ellen Hepworth. Born 20 October 1938. Which makes her a Libran and that's all I know about her. Not a photograph, nothing. And believe me, I looked.'

'Have a drink. Have a glass of red.'

He filled two glasses from the wine cask and brought them to the table. Remorseful, now, he said, 'It's nothing to be ashamed of.'

'It is where I come from. George the Third. The History teacher taught us that: George the Third should simply never have occurred. He didn't know, of course. The class did, though, and a couple of them tried to get my eye.'

'I think you could be imagining that.'

'Maybe. It wouldn't have been so bad if the family hadn't thought so much of themselves to begin with. The story was that everything started to go downhill with Gran Mary and her daughters were bad blood.' She grinned. 'Grace was bad blood all right. I think Grace was their punishment for what they did to Nora.'

'What did they do to Nora?'

'Turned her out, took me away from her. Then Grace started her career. Scandal they didn't want, Grace gave them scandal, all right. They tried too hard to cover up, got rid of Nora, tried to pass me off as Alice's. She'd have been the only one young enough to have another baby. Clare's four years older than I am.'

'You mean that they passed you off as Alice's child? How could they get away with it?' Though he knew from his practice that families could make very strange arrangements.

'They were a fair way out of town. Just kept out of sight, I suppose, and went to Newcastle for the birth. They didn't even tell me that Nora was my mother, but I knew. They'd be talking about Nora, then see me and drop their voices, or say "Little pitchers have big ears", and shut up.

'It didn't take, either, trying to cover up. Alice was so annoyed at being lumbered with me that she told everybody. I didn't even know she was supposed to be my mother till I saw my birth certificate. Applying for a scholarship. If you knew how it bugs me having that bitch's name on my birth certificate. For a while I thought she must be, really, because it was written there. Official. It seemed worse, if I really was her child and she'd written me off. There wasn't anybody I could ask; I knew by that time it was something to shut up about. I thought I must have done something terrible before I could remember. But that went. I knew it didn't make sense. It was just a shock, seeing it written there.'

'Your dinner's getting cold.'

She nodded and began to eat. When she pushed her empty glass to him, he realised she had forgotten about feeding Walt. Well, once wouldn't hurt him. He'd survive.

He filled her glass for her.

'A charming childhood.'

'It wasn't so bad. Doreen was like a mother, really. She liked looking after me, it never seemed to be a chore. It was a blow when she married, but I could get by then and the other girls were all right. It was a bit awkward being Uncle Clyde's favourite, because it gave Alice a handle. Doing for that child what you don't do for your own. But when you're young you accept things. Most of the time things just went along. Funny, after Doreen left I used to want to go and live with Grace.'

'But I thought Grace . . .'

'Yes, she was. But that was why, you see. I could have looked after the children, washed their clothes, cleaned the place up.'

She spoke with real exasperation, as if dirt and disorder were worse than moral delinquency. She certainly cleaned and polished all surfaces in her own house. Perhaps she thought of the body beautiful as an area that had to be kept in perfect order, like the kitchen. He could see that in Grace's home she would have been a paragon.

'Not that I saw much of Grace, but I heard plenty.'

'Heard what, exactly?'

'Oh, it was Fred, really. He's a bit of a crim, in a refined sort of way, fraud and such. I don't know the details but he did a stretch in Maitland, and Grace on welfare and forever begging . . . and yet in a way so respectable.' Though weary, she grinned. 'I think she thought she was a worthy cause.'

'I've met the type.' That was a moment for hope.

'So I had this idea, you see, of coming to the rescue.'

'A change from being George the Third.'

'Yes. Like Florence Nightingale. Then one day Grace came to the house, it must have been when things weren't so bad, Fred must have been working, because I heard — by that time I had long ears, I suppose — I heard Alice say, "Are you ever going to do your duty by that child, Grace?" That child, in that tone of voice, was me.'

She paused, breathed deeply. He thought she might weep, but she went on calmly, 'She said, "I hardly think Fred would like it." Fred's weakness for crime was a sort of interesting disease, to Grace. He had to have special consideration.'

'But why should you have been Grace's duty, in any case?' No use commenting on the rest of it, being despised by the despicable. No words for that.

'Well, she was my real aunt, wasn't she? Alice was only a half-aunt, she would have brooded on that.' She admitted, 'That still bites, that I wasn't good enough for Grace.'

'I should think it all still bites, and no wonder. But that's just human nature, isn't it, after all? Grace was despised by all, she had to have someone to despise.'

She nodded minimally.

'But you got out.'

'After what Alice said about the dance dress. Like mother, like daughter was the least of it. Said I'd got it out of Uncle Clyde by . . . oh, never mind.'

He nodded, silent in horror.

'Poor uncle, I was so embarrassed, so was he, I suppose. He drove me over to Auntie Em's, never said a word on the way. And I was holding the box with the dress, sitting in the front of the utility, dumb, holding this box with the damned dress in it, the things you remember, like being thrown out into the night with a baby . . . oh, hell!'

'You know your cousin said it wasn't for you but against Alice. There'd always been trouble between them.'

'There was trouble between them after that all right. I don't think they ever spoke to each other again. Alice went to stay with Doreen and didn't come back; Clare kept house for Uncle Clyde.'

'You never saw him again?'

'He died suddenly, of a heart attack. I got news, I've always kept in touch with Doreen. She's no sort of letter writer but I see to it she knows where I am. I wouldn't have wanted to see him again, we were both too embarrassed.' She frowned, sighed and said irritably, 'End of story.'

That left him high and dry, wanting to show sympathy, not knowing how. She was unapproachable, wouldn't thank him to get up and put his arm round her.

He said, 'Not an easy life,' but words were weak; they didn't reach her. He had his own burden; married nearly three years and he hadn't known this. A terrible gulf had become visible.

'I'll get the coffee.'

'There's some of that mousse left from yesterday, if you want it.'

He shook his head. How tired he was! She must be exhausted. She drank her coffee in silence. He offered to clear away and wash up. She said briefly, 'No, leave it!'

He thought she would be better alone. He went to his desk, to the work he had brought home from chambers but drowsed over it to no purpose, so he gave up and went to bed, where he fell asleep at once.

He woke in daylight. Ann was lying awake, staring at nothing in stony despair. At once he was queasy with dread. He got up and went straight to Walt's room. He was asleep, healthy and peaceful, head on one side, fists raised in the usual double Fascist salute. Looking down at him in deep relief, Bill thought, 'Nothing else can harm me.'

But what was eating Ann?

He went into the kitchen, where he found a small scene of drunken disorder, washing-up half done, a broken glass in a puddle of wine on the draining board. The wine cask was on the kitchen table; he lifted it and felt its lightness. Ann, alone in the kitchen, had gone on the drink.

And who had left her alone in that desperate frame of mind? A fine start.

He cleaned up the mess, finished the washing-up, made tea and carried it into the bedroom, a silent sign that he had seen the mess in the kitchen and was not censorious but apologetic. Since he rarely made the tea, that added to the atmosphere of crisis. He put her cup on the table beside her; she looked at it and looked away, fixed in misery.

He asked, fishing, 'When did you feed him?'

'He slept through till five. And just as well,' she shouted, 'Because I was drunk. I was too drunk to cope. I might have dropped him. Dropped him on his head or crippled him.' She was aghast. He too had turned cold at the thought.

'He said at length, 'It didn't happen, did it?'

'It could have.'

He sat on the bed drinking his tea and looking for arguments. 'Look, I don't think so. There are instincts that take care of such things.' But did she have them? It was a moot point. 'Besides, situations are never so clear cut. If you'd been so incapable, you wouldn't have woken up, would you?' Was that why she was so rigid in perfection, because she didn't have instinct to guide her? Like those monkeys trapped in infancy who haven't learnt mothering? 'Walt would have screamed till I woke. I would have woken you, we would have made up one sober soul between us. Besides, I knew you were upset, I shouldn't have left you alone. It was my fault.'

So it was, but with an angry shrug of her whole body, she denied it.

The damned thing was that with Ann looking like a stranger, with the atmosphere of guilt and disorder and a touch of hangover headache, he felt a worm of adulterous desire stir and stiffen in him. That disconcerted him, because he knew it would shock her. Unthinkable, except in the dark on the two regular nights a week.

'Come on, sit up and drink your tea. It didn't happen, did it? So forget it.'

'You're shocked, aren't you?'

'You're not the first who ever had a few drinks.'

'That's not what I mean.'

He prevaricated.

'You haven't done anything to be shocked about, have you?' He said gallantly, 'I think you've come out of it very well.' He didn't know if that was true. Primness and rigidity might be worse than wildness.

What an odd look she had on her face! He had noticed it when Bridie mentioned the toilet paper ad stuck on the old woman's bedroom wall: she looked as if she had something in her mouth that tasted strange and was making up her mind whether or not she liked it.

At breakfast he said, 'What about coming to watch the game today? Get out in the air. Come for the morning session and I'll bring you home at lunch time. Walt should last that long.'

'I have a few things to do in the house.' She added bitterly, 'I'm not going to get drunk.'

'Oh, for God's sake! Who ever said you would? And I wish you would get some help in the house. You don't have to spend your life scrubbing and polishing.'

'They never do it properly.'

'Well, try to relax a bit. Don't do too much.'

He made fifty-two and would still be in if the umpire hadn't been one-eyed. He came home physically tired and mentally relaxed and thought, when he found the house neat and shining, the table set, Walt in his carry-chair waving and beaming recognition, that the appearance of happiness could take one a long way. He unstrapped the baby and lifted him to his shoulder, murmuring, 'Good day, my mate.'

Ann looked in from the kitchen doorway. 'He's pretty lively. Walk him about a bit, will you? Get him a bit tired, if you can.'

He walked into the garden with the baby, tossed him, talked to him, walked him about till he began to yawn and sag. As he laid him in his cot and tucked the blanket round him, he thought, 'To make a happy home for you, there's nothing I wouldn't do. If I knew how.' Knowing how was the thing.

'Well, he's gone off. Out like a light.'

'That's good.' She was sitting at the kitchen table, drinking the one whisky she allowed herself before dinner. She must really be needing it, considering last night's excesses, if she had hung out till then. 'He had about an hour this afternoon, been awake ever since, so he might sleep through.' He wished she wouldn't talk about Walt as if he was a business she was running.

'How did the game go?'

'We're ahead on the first innings.' He would feel a fool, telling her he had made fifty-two. 'What have you done today?'

'Washed the woodwork, cleaned the silver, took him for a walk in the park.'

Doing a Lady Macbeth scrub-up, maybe. He said, 'Ann . . .' meaning to talk about other ways of spending Saturday, but she cut him short.

'I've decided I want to go. For that weekend at the farm. I've been thinking about it.' That explained the gloss on the silver. 'I'm going to ask Aunt Em where my mother is.'

'Jesus, Ann, no. Don't do it.' He felt such fear for her, it was like love. 'Don't go digging . . . Sometimes, it's just better not to know.'

'I have the right to know.'

No. Keep your Nora. Born under Libra, he remembered with a pang of sympathy. Keep your romantic, unfortunate Nora.

How could he convince her that even if the reality wasn't bad — and there was no guarantee of that — it could never match what she'd built for herself?

'You might not like what you find.'

'I've thought of that. I still want to know.'

He sighed. 'OK. It's your decision, but I wish you wouldn't.'

He tried again during dinner.

'You do realise that she could always have found you if she had wanted to?'

'Oh, I know that. But she would have thought, you see, that I didn't know anything about her. So far as she knew, I thought Alice was my mother. She wouldn't have done me any favour by turning up.'

'No, I see.'

If only she wouldn't talk as if she were privy to Nora's thoughts. It was hard to believe, listening to her, that she'd never met Nora and knew nothing about her.

I wonder if she reads her horoscope. Poor little coot.

Gavin was excited to learn that there were platypus in the river. He would very much like to see platypus living free in their habitat.

'He means,' said Colin solemnly, 'in the water.'

'Now, that isn't the whole story, you know.'

'They don't come when they're called,' said Bridie. 'You have to know where to find them.'

Her mother suggested, 'Why don't you go and see George? He'd know.'

George was their old bachelor neighbour, who spent his days in his garden or along the river.

She added, 'I've got a few things to send over to him, too.'

So, late on Saturday afternoon, Gavin carrying a carton with jam, pickles and cake, he and Bridie took the road to George's house. They found him sitting on his back step disentangling a fishing-line. He was a small, sturdy, gnarled man with the unused face of a puppet left out long in the weather.

'Ah, Bridie!' George gave a shy, sidewise nod to Gavin as he took the carton.

'A few things Mum sent over.'

'Tell her the fish are running. I'll be out early tomorrow, bring her a feed of fish if my luck's in.'

'Great. I'll tell her. We've got Annie coming tomorrow, with her husband and baby. Remember Annie?'

'The tall, fair one from the other house? Time gets on.'

'Sure does. Are there any platypus about in the river, George? Gavin's never seen them, outside the zoo.'

George was silent, consulting his mental map of the river. 'Tell you what, you're going the wrong way. Down behind your own place, past the swimming hole. There's a colony comes out most evenings. You should be right. Got a torch?'

'Didn't think of it.'

'Won't get far, will you?'

'Feel like coming with us, showing us the spot?'

'Might as well. I'll get me torch, then.'

Gavin was disappointed. He had cherished the thought of sitting alone with Bridie on the river bank, watching the platypus. But Bridie knew best; this was her territory. They followed the old man diagonally across the fields, uphill and down, to their own familiar stretch of river, past the ford, where the water ran shining and broken over round stones, along the flat grassed bank past stiller, deeper water to the swimming hole and beyond, where the river narrowed.

'Here we are.' George spoke quietly. 'Can you see that clump hanging over near the water? That's where the burrow mouth is, right under it. Can't see it from here but that's where they'll come from if they're coming.'

They sat in silence waiting for the dark. The air was so still that they heard the old man draw his breath, then a slight plop and a ripple, then another. Gavin peered; in the twilight, it was like watching pure motion. The old man switched on the torch. He had caught one of the animals in its circle of light: a duckbill bearded with ripples, a swift fish-like dart away. The light went out. 'Well, that's your platypus.'

Gavin said, 'Thanks. That was wonderful.'

'Cunning little beggars, they are. Make the entrance to the burrow real tight, so they squeegee the water out of their fur on the way in, get home dry. It's wonderful how they think of it.'

'We'd better be getting back,' said Bridie.

'You'd have got a better look if I'd caught you one.'

They walked by the light of the torch now, along the bank.

'You're not netting, are you, George?'

'Lord, no. Your Dad would have my scalp. Some still netting, though. You get a platypus caught in your net, you're in trouble. They turn real nasty and it's the devil getting them out.' Triumph was making the old man talkative, though the uphill walk made him struggle for breath. 'Eh, you know Jock Williams, Bridie? Old fellow along Dulapin, up the river? He was netting around here and took a platypus. Hard to handle, got this poison fang behind the back leg. Trying to get it out, it got him in the thumb.' He chuckled. 'Put up with it a couple of days, thumb black and big as a sausage and giving him misery, so he has to go to the doc with it. Netting being illegal, see, so he couldn't say he got it in a net. Says he took it on a line, got stung trying to get it off the hook. Doc Stevens, he's crazy about such things, wants to know what bait, what time of day, the lot. Writes off to this magazine about the first platypus taken on a line. Got it printed and all. Came and showed it to Jock. Jock couldn't hardly keep his face straight.'

Gavin lost the mild elation the sight of the platypus had brought. A lie, he thought, and in a *scientific journal*. He must do something about it. He must talk to Bridie. They said goodbye to the old man when they reached the dairy and hurried downhill towards the lighted house. There wasn't breath or time to talk about it.

He knew his devotion to truth was excessive, even neurotic. He knew where it came from; it was reaction against his poor maddening mother, throwing the bright cloak of her dreams over dismal reality, suffering such pain when reality as ever showed through. He knew this but he could not help himself. Truth was a compulsion. When he was younger, he used to lie awake thinking of Galileo, not with disapproval — of course, facing the Inquisition's fire, a man would lie and save his skin — but with fear. Suppose one couldn't find the words, couldn't bring out the saving lie? And then the fire . . .

He'd never been asked to die for a great truth but he had suffered for small ones. Girlfriend after girlfriend . . . women — all women until he met Bridie — had wanted a tribute he couldn't pay. He hadn't understood that clearly until Natalie, who was an intellectual, and of whom he had had hopes, had greeted him with 'Old Silver Tongue himself!' said with a cheerful amusement that had shown him he would never be looked on as a lover. He had given up and lived lonely until he met Bridie.

He had no chance to discuss the letter with her until he was lying in bed, watching her take the pins out of her hair at the dressing table.

'Bridie, that letter about the platypus — I think we ought to do something about it.'

She turned her face to him, half shocked and half laughing. 'You don't want to grass on the poor old fellow, do you?'

'I don't want to make trouble for him, but after all it's a scientific journal . . .'

At the word *scientific* she became respectful. 'What do you want to do about it?'

'One could write and point out that netting is illegal at the point where the platypus was taken, but that there is some evidence that it is practised.'

'There sure is that.'

'Well, that doesn't accuse anyone. It offers relevant information that hasn't been taken into account.'

'You don't know George. It could have happened two years ago. Maybe more. He'll still be telling the story ten years from now. We'd have to find out what magazine and how long ago. I suppose we could find out from silly old Stevens. We'll have to work out a good cover story, though.' She looked as if she would find that amusing.

He went blank with shock.

'But I do think a scientist would take it with a grain of salt. It's only an old man's yarn.'

'Yes. I suppose you're right.'

He felt giddy, disoriented, as if a marble pillar he had been leaning on had dissolved into cloud. Yet the cloud held him. If he had been deceived in Bridie, he was glad of it.

She put out the light and climbed in beside him. The mattress billowed round him, like the cloud. It made a hill between them which for once he welcomed.

The first image of her, the moment of true seeing which had been the beginning of love — how had it convinced him, at once and completely, that she was incapable of lying? She had been standing at the scales, weighing out the rats' food, careful, quick and attentive. At her elbow scrawny Liz, eaten by an inward hunger, always begging for praise, holding open a fashion magazine: 'Do you think this would suit me?' Bridie had turned to look at the photograph with the same careful attention and answered, 'I don't think you have the height for it.' So clear, precise, so black and white she was, the black hair neat in a bun, the white lab coat padded as jolly as a Christmas stocking; that turn of the head had revealed the pure profile and the solid white neck — an unassuming beauty of which he thought he was the discoverer.

What in that image had made him suppose she could not lie? Not suppose — it was an absolute joyful certainty. Why? The question was too difficult, the mattress soft and sustaining. He fell asleep.

On Sunday morning Bridie's Gran took the breakfast scraps to the fowls and coming back paused with the empty pail under the crabapple tree. Annie's tree, it was, in her mind. She had paused there, getting on thirty years ago, to look at Annie in her pram and found her looking up to the sky and laughing quietly to herself. The feeling that had started in Em she could never name or explain — it was like fright, the laughter being against nature, astonishing, like a spring of water running out of dead, naked ground. Alice and poor weepy Gran Mary had been rowing in the kitchen and that baby was lying there gurgling with joy.

'What have you got to laugh about, I'd like to know?' Em had cried in anger, or anguish, and the baby had stopped laughing, drawn a tight little crab face and started to cry. She had picked it up then, talked to it softly, stroked and patted it till it began to smile again. She had walked with it into the kitchen and said, 'You can stop your arguing. I'll take her myself.' She had been forced to that, willing or unwilling, since she had heard the laughter.

They had both turned on her, as she might have known,

asking what good that would do — if Alice, who was as wicked as a decent woman could be, didn't want the baby, she certainly wanted a reason to torment Mary, and she had it and wasn't going to let go of it.

Em had given in, had carried the baby back to its pram and settled it down, feeling relieved that she'd been forced to it. She hadn't looked forward to the work, bottles and napkins and broken sleep — she'd been a bit old for it and had only the two men in the house, while Alice had the four girls. It had seemed to be for the best, since Doreen took to the little thing and was like a mother to her, till the night when Clyde brought Annie over, both of them white and dazed with shock (and guilt? She didn't believe it, never would believe it, but when a thing like that was said, it hung about like a smell.), Clyde had said there was a bit of trouble in the house, but their faces said more, everyone hushed and scurrying as if it was a death. Annie had stopped laughing, all right, but Em didn't think then about the baby under the crabapple tree; her mind was full of what had happened, or hadn't happened. It was much later, seeing her in the magazine, beautiful as an angel in her fluffy nightgown, with her hands up to catch that ribbon of toilet paper — Ellen had said, 'Look! That's Annie!' and pushed the magazine across to her — beautiful but far away, not belonging to this world. Then Em had remembered the baby and told herself she had given up too easily. It had been up to her. She was the one who had heard the laughter; she should have guarded it.

What she wanted was not so much to see Annie before she died as to hear her laugh, to lay that ghost.

Well, she was coming, this afternoon, with her husband and her own baby. That should settle it.

Gavin and Bridie came out when they heard the car stop. Ann getting out put her finger to her lips; Walt was asleep in his capsule. Gavin lifted him out while Bridie gave Bill directions for parking the car; meanwhile a small, weathered, brightly coloured old woman had come out on to the verandah and stood waiting silently. Like a burning bush, thought Bill as he advanced with the luggage — the clash of fading auburn hair

with sun-reddened skin put that into his head. This must be the
Aunt Em who could not die happy until she had seen Ann
again, but no one would think it from her manner. Ann, in
embarrassment, overdid the greeting, put both hands out in a
real actress gesture, said 'Auntie Em!' and kissed her on the
cheek, then froze as the old woman ducked her head. So they
stood.

'And this is Bill.'

She ducked her head again, this time in greeting, then looked
into the capsule and smiled her satisfaction at the contents.
'You've got a fine boy there, Annie.'

'We think so.'

'Come on in,' said Bridie. 'We'll put your things in your
room. Mum's got afternoon tea ready. You'll be wanting a cup.'

The room to which she led them seemed to Bill a period
piece: iron bedstead, white honeycomb quilt, tall cedar chest of
drawers bearing a mirror in a swinging frame.

Bridie saw his thought in his eyes. 'Kept it all so long,' she
murmured, 'it's back in fashion. You brought the folding cot?'

'It's in the boot.'

Walt was still asleep. They left him in his capsule on the bed.
The old woman was not to be seen. Ann walked ahead of them,
alone and tense, into the kitchen.

The woman (Bridie's mother — that leapt to the eye) was
standing at a table spread as for a wedding breakfast.

'Well, Annie!'

'Ellen.'

They rubbed cheeks.

'And you'll be Bill. And where's the baby?'

'He's asleep. We left him in his capsule on the bed.'

The old woman had appeared again at the door. 'Strapped in
like one of those spacemen.'

Bill said, 'We don't keep him in a straightjacket. It's just for
safety in the car.'

'I've seen a few that could do with a straightjacket, at that.
Well, sit down and have a cup of tea.'

Ellen managed the conversation, handing remarks while she
handed the sandwiches. 'You haven't changed much, Annie.

You don't look a day older, really. Got your figure back. Are you breastfeeding? Ah, that takes it off you. Bridie says you're a lawyer, Bill? I wish we could have kept Colin to his books.' Passing Gavin his third slice of cake, she said cheerfully, 'I wonder where you put it all.'

'I have a very high metabolic rate,' said Gavin.

'I think you get poor carrying it about.'

Gavin swallowed his chewed mouthful. 'That is another way of putting it, yes.' He was at ease, eating his third slice. Ellen's detached good humour was solid ground to walk on.

When the women began to clear away, Bill said, 'Shall I check on him?' and was off when Ann nodded to the bedroom where Walt lay in his capsule looking about him with the alertness that was a sure sign of high intelligence.

Controlling his face to conceal pride Bill carried him back to the kitchen and to cries of 'Oh, the little love!' 'Look at his bright eyes!'

Ellen took him from Bill and talked nonsense to him; his small face gathered itself into a scowl, then he wailed, looking about him till he found Ann and leaned towards her with his arms outstretched. For a moment she stood staring; astonishment sparked in her eyes, spread and took hold. What should follow was joy; what came was trouble, dread and uncertainty.

'You don't want anyone but your Mum, do you? Off you go, then.'

Ann took the boy willingly but appeared inscrutable.

Bill thought, 'She wants to give him everything, be the perfect mother. Poor girl. This is one thing she can't get out of the books.' He was seized by real pity and was startled to find the emotion so different from other varieties that bore its name.

'What about a walk?' said Gavin. 'I need to walk off all that cake.' He perceived with vexation that he was playing games. Bold about his appetite, he was shy about his romantic love for the farm, knowing it must seem absurd and trivial to the men who worked the land, the possessors and possessed.

'Yes, go on then,' said Ellen. 'Annie'd like to look around, wouldn't you?'

They set off, Bill carrying Walt, Ann his blanket, Gavin in silence contemplating the broad ordered fields in the calm of late afternoon, Bridie walking with Ann recalling the past.

'Do you remember the cubby house, Annie? It used to be over there in the corner. Dad knocked it down when I went away. I created when I came back and found it was gone.'

'I was too big to fit in,' said Ann. 'I had to be the outside character huffing and puffing. You and Colin were the little pigs.'

'And looking through the window growling, being the wicked giant.'

'But Colin got really frightened. I had a time calming him down.'

'Fairy stories are frightening.' Bill was considering this new view of Ann, huffing and puffing outside the cubby house. 'I think they must be intended as a preparation for the worst the world can do.' Looking down at Walt, he felt anger and sadness that the world must disappoint his expectations, at the best. At the worst . . . 'Did you play together much, then? There's a fair age gap.'

Ann was repressive now. 'I was minding them while Doreen and Ellen went to town.'

They had reached the dairy. Bridie took them in to pay their respects to the rotolactor and was pleased to see Ann's eyes widen.

'Times have changed!'

'Times have changed all right. Everything up to date in Kansas city.'

Bill was still occupied with the unexpected picture of Ann playing with the small children. Was there hope then? Had she been role playing, or was there some warmth there? Warmth seemed to linger for Bridie and it seemed to him now and then that she warmed to Bridie still.

Now they were looking down at the river, discussing whether they should go further. Bill gazed. The sunlight was breaking sharp on the shallow water of the ford; further upstream the water ran deep and calm between rising banks.

'What a backyard!' said Bill. 'Imagine owning it.'

Gavin nodded in sympathy.

Ann agreed, 'Yes, it's a pretty spot.'

'We walked along to the swimming hole last night with George to have a look at the platypus.'

The conversation lapsed. The view induced silence.

Bill took the blanket from Ann and wrapped it round Walt. It was a signal. They turned and walked back towards the house.

Gavin asked, 'Do you ever miss the country, Ann?'

'Yes. Now that I see it again, I realise how much . . . but I'd miss the city more, I think.'

'The country looks a lot better than it is,' said Bridie.

Gavin was silent. His love for this land was not to be spoken of. It was like an innocent passion for another man's wife.

Bridie had been sitting with Ann while she fed Walt. Now she came into the kitchen carrying him, saying, 'Look at me! I've been promoted,' but at that moment Walt cried and struggled towards Ann as she came in behind them. 'Oh, well!' she said cheerfully as she handed him over, 'He'll know me and love me yet.'

Ellen was standing at the stove, Gran sat close by stringing beans into a colander, Gavin and Bill sat at the table drinking beer.

'Where's Dad, Mum? He's in late, isn't he?'

'Gone over to Charlie's to look at a sick tractor. Charlie's never heard about garages.'

'Heard about money, though,' said Gran.

'Speak of the devil!'

A truck drew up outside. In a moment the two tall men came in, bringing two kinds of silence. In young Colin, lurking behind his father, it came from a shyness that was endearing in a handsome eighteen-year-old; it was different with his father, who stood blank-faced, rigid with the shame of an unforgotten scandal.

Ann had her social manner on at once, smiled easily, said, 'Hullo, Malcolm. It's been a long time, hasn't it? You haven't changed much. Colin, I don't suppose you remember me.'

Malcolm gave a sick smile which died at once.

'Of course he remembers you,' said Ellen. 'Annie used to mind you, plenty of times.'

'I used to give you a pickaback when you were too tired to walk.' She looked at the length of him, deliberately charming — who could blame her? 'I wouldn't like to try it now.'

'You can if you like.' Colin blushed, then grinned.

Malcolm meanwhile was getting beer out of the fridge. 'Well, who's drinking?'

Ellen said quickly, 'Bridie and I will have a sherry. What about you, Ann?'

Ann nodded. 'That will suit me.'

Whether they were protecting Ann from Malcolm or Malcolm from Ann, they took the situation for granted and showed no indignation. That was left to Bill. During dinner he found out what it must be like to be George the Third. The worst of it was that Malcolm tried. He was suffering, not aggressive. He directed a few questions about the journey and the state of the roads into the narrow gap between Bill and Ann. Since Bill, who was saying to himself in rage, 'My *wife!* My *wife!* Who does he think he is?' chose to ignore the questions, Ann was forced to recognise her own existence and answer briefly. She didn't seem to be indignant, either. 'Get angry!' Bill said to her in his mind, but the message didn't reach her.

Under this strain, the conversation died. Though Bill could have sworn that the women were sympathetic to Ann, they did not recognise her existence either. Even Bridie ignored her. Gavin looked troubled, Colin kept his eyes down. To speak to Ann would be to take a position.

If Bill hadn't seen it, he would never have believed it. He felt like shouting, 'For God's sake, look at her! Is she such a blot on the landscape? Doesn't she have the right to live?'

Enlightenment came with that thought. Over roast lamb and fruit salad and cream, he digested Ann's obsession with her appearance, her passport to living.

He looked at Walt, who was lying in his carry chair chirruping quietly as he batted at the knitted doll suspended in front of him. Sadly he thought, 'Why aren't you enough? Why don't you give her her papers?'

He didn't ask himself why he didn't. It was too painful a question.

He hadn't been speaking to Ann himself. That would have made the situation more obvious. Ellen spoke now and then to Malcolm: 'How did you go with the truck?' 'Roy Paterson rang. He wants you to ring him back tonight.'

It was Malcolm's table. Ellen paid tribute, though as sparely as possible. Tea in the farmhouse kitchen proceeded with the formality of dinner at Versailles, and everyone took it for granted, except possibly Gavin, who was not in a position to defy protocol.

Bill followed Ann when she got up to take Walt to bed. He said furiously as soon as they reached the bedroom, 'What's eating him? Great manners I must say.'

Ann had laid Walt on the bed and was peeling off his jumpsuit. She said calmly, 'I suppose he believes it. About me and Uncle Clyde.'

'No sane person could believe that.'

'People always believe it, when it's sex. Even if they don't believe it, they blame you for making them think about it.' She looked up. Though her voice was calm, her face was burning red. 'He was my father. Up to then I had a father. He made a fuss of me because I was the youngest, and I suppose a bit more because Alice didn't. I called him Uncle but the way I thought — I suppose you'd say a father figure.'

'It's hard enough to imagine your parents having sex at all, isn't it? Let alone . . .'

He was nervous, intent on saying the right thing, thinking that even the wrong thing was better than silence.

'With oneself, yes.' She got that out with a gasp and was, he thought, relieved. The right thing. 'Alice didn't believe it, though. Not for a minute. She just got so mad about the evening dress that she threw the worst thing she could think of. She worked herself up and up until she said it and you could see, once it was out, she was frightened.'

Walt's napkin was off and he was kicking furiously. It was time for a game. He fixed his eyes on Bill and squawked in anger. Bill caught a foot, held it and tickled it, making him squeal with joy.

'What a thoroughly delightful woman.'

She nodded, safety pins in mouth, as she tried to bring Walt and napkin together. Bill caught both feet and held them; Walt gave in to fate with a grizzle.

'None of that.' Ann put him into his pyjamas and laid him in the folding cot. While she tucked him in, Bill said, 'I don't feel like staying. I feel like going home now. Why should you put up with it?'

Ann looked astonished. 'You wouldn't get far if you worried about that sort of thing. You get used to it.' With an odd comic grimace she added, 'You don't have much choice.'

Get angry! he begged silently. Don't accept it. Get angry!
'OK. But how do we get through the evening?'

After all, the evening turned out well. By the time they had settled Walt down, Malcolm and Colin were in the living room in front of the television set, the women were finishing the washing up and Gavin was sitting at the kitchen table waiting for them.

'Do you fancy a game of Scrabble?'

Time was for killing. Bill agreed, Ann didn't know the game but was persuaded to learn. Gavin fetched the set from the living room and they sat down to play.

After the oppressive atmosphere of dinner, spirits rebounded. Both men were keen players, Bridie was slower and Ann was tentative. Gavin noted conscientiously that he was enjoying the game more because the men were superior, though he deplored the weakness. Bill and Ann went down after Ann had carelessly opened the way for Gavin to a triple word score. She sat dejected through the closing rounds till Bill, who was beginning to learn his way, said, 'It's a game. We don't get shot for losing.'

'We gloat a little, that's all,' said Gavin as he calculated the scores.

They played again; Colin had come out to watch and was straddling a chair between Bill and Bridie. The old woman sat in the corner, idle and quiet as a domestic cat.

Bill arranged his first seven letters and began to laugh; Colin looked over his shoulder and roared with glee.

'Full of filth, this game, like the dictionary. I could have scored a fifty bonus for that.'

'Put it down, go on.'

'No.' He picked up the letters, threw them into the bag and drew seven more. 'I pass.'

'More fool you.' Bridie took the first turn.

'If we lose I claim a moral victory.'

'A bad loser I can stand. A sanctimonious bad loser is a little too much.' Gavin studied the board with attention.

Sometimes the little silver ball rolls into the socket: happiness. Bill couldn't imagine why he should be happy but there it was, a moment of holiday.

Bill and Ann won the second game. Ann said then that it was time to check on Walt. After her departure, the silent admirers, the young man and the old woman, disappeared too. Bridie watched while Gavin and Bill played a decider, which failed to decide. They closed up the board and were glad to abandon the game when Ellen came out to get the supper.

Ann joined them in the living room, where she was invisible again. Malcolm drinking his tea kept his eyes fixed on the television screen; all, except Bridie — even the old woman — pretended not to see her. Bridie made room for her on the sofa, poured her tea and asked about milk and sugar in a carefully lowered voice. Bill perceived that Ann was right: one did get used to it. He was beginning to accept her invisibility himself, tried to decide if he should speak to her and decided it wasn't worth while making a demonstration.

After supper, bed. He wondered if some bottled-up emotion would keep Ann awake. Himself, he would be seething — was seething indeed on her account, but she went calmly to sleep. It was her acceptance that chilled him most. She was that character in the Greek myths, the one with the stinking wound: his name was . . . Phyl . . . something . . . Then it was daylight.

It seemed that Ann was after all to receive a family heirloom. At midmorning Ellen came into the kitchen, where the two couples sat chatting.

'Gran wants to see you in the front room, Annie.'

Ann said, 'No!'

Bridie and Ellen looked at each other in dismay.

'It means a lot to Gran, Annie.'

'I don't want any of your great-grandmother's things. She wasn't my great-grandmother, was she?'

Ellen said, 'You can take some little thing, surely. You have to humour her a bit, Annie. She's old. Be old yourself some day.'

Bridie added, 'You'd break her up. She feels a lot more than you'd think.'

Ann nodded, suddenly. They set off in procession for the front room.

It was of an earlier period than the rest of the house, thick-walled, stone-floored, with an open fireplace, a rag rug, a rocking-chair varnished black and bearing a cretonne cushion. The only modern piece of furniture was a large glass-fronted cabinet with old china and silver ranged on the shelves. The central position on the central shelf was occupied by a tall vase, bright in royal blue and gold, with an oval inset of pastel shepherdesses. Sèvres, all right, thought Bill. The old woman stood beside the cabinet, formal as if she was about to make a speech — an odd notion, that. The rest grouped in front of her just as formally, Ann in front, Bill at her elbow studying the contents of the cabinet and wondering how Ann rated — a teacup, perhaps?

The old woman opened the cabinet. It was the Sèvres vase she took in her hands. As she turned, Ann said quickly, 'Auntie Em, where's my mother? I want you to tell me where my mother is.' While Em gaped at her, she added, 'Oh, I know Nora is my mother. Nobody told me, but I always knew.'

The vase leapt out of Em's hands and broke against the stone floor.

Everyone stood transfixed and stared at the pieces. Ann put her hands to her mouth, muffling a scream. Em stopped staring, grinned and said, 'Well, that fixes Alice. Now don't get into a taking, Annie. It's a good riddance.' She crouched with slow, difficult movements to pick up the pieces, then said, 'Nora's dead, Annie. Been dead a long time.'

Well, that was true. As she put pieces of china together in a heap, she was putting together pieces of the past. Poor Nora (birth injury, nothing in the family) — it was that very year of Annie's birth that poor Nora had to be put away. Em had blamed the rows, the shrieking and crying in the house that had turned poor Nora violent. If Mary hadn't been so wrapped up in Nora all her life, Grace might have turned out better, but it was a hard punishment for her.

Watching the old woman, thinking that something was costing her dear, whether it was regret for the vase or for Nora's fate, Bill had a sudden widening of consciousness, perceiving love in the giving mode, dogged, enduring, self-effacing — his portion, his destiny. He hadn't chosen it, it was the last thing he would have chosen.

Ann's hands were covering her mouth still, tears were rolling down her face. She turned and hurried out of the room.

Bill said, 'I'm sorry. About the vase. If I can do anything — get it riveted . . .'

'Forget it,' said Ellen. 'Best thing that ever happened.' Yet she too sounded shocked and flustered.

Em got to her feet. She said abruptly to Bill, 'Go after Annie.'

'Yes. She's had a bad shock. You understand, to her, she's just lost her mother.'

When he had gone, Ellen said, 'Would have been a worse shock if she'd found her.'

Em nodded, finding nothing to say.

Bridie looked down at the remains of the vase. 'I'd better get a dustpan. I don't feel like putting it out with the garbage. We ought to give it a decent burial.'

Ellen laughed, accepting Fate's strange quirks.

'Elaine and Alice can have half each. Look, we'll keep the pieces, just in case they don't believe us. There's an empty shoebox in the pantry, love. Go and fetch it, will you, and the dustpan.'

Gavin followed Bridie to the kitchen.

'She meant to give it to Ann, didn't she?'

'Yes. Poor Annie. It would have been the evening dress all over again. And worse.'

'Ann stopped her. You could see her warding it off.'

'Pretty good, Annie must be, at warding things off.'

'It's nothing to laugh about, Bridie. She's grieving for her mother, that's natural.'

'Where this shoebox is . . .'

Bridie had advanced into the pantry. Gavin came to the door. She looked back at him and made a decision.

'Nora was no more Annie's mother than I am,' she muttered.

Gavin gaped. 'Who is, then?'

'Grace is, of course.' Bridie sounded angry. 'I don't know how Annie has lived so long without finding that out. Oh, here's the shoebox.'

'Who was Nora, then?'

'Hush, love. Keep your voice down. Nora was brain-damaged, lived at home till she was grown up, I think. She was Grace's sister. Mum always said that was what went wrong with Grace, that her mother was so wrapped up in Nora, Grace had to go to the bad to get any attention. But she certainly kept on going once she'd started. Nora was put away, she was just a name. It was all hushed up. I was the original little pitcher with the big ears, I can remember when Nora died.' She shook her head. 'I don't know where Annie got that idea. Come on, we'd better get back. They'll think we're making the shoebox.'

'Once Ann had the idea fixed in her mind, she would interpret evidence accordingly. I can see that.'

Bridie smiled. 'I like it. Grace rejected her, so she rejected Grace. Like, you can't sack me, I resign.'

'I wonder how the truth would affect her now.'

They were close to the front room. Bridie said in a quick fierce whisper, 'I wouldn't thank anyone who told her.'

So now Gavin had his own private lie to cherish. He couldn't help seeing a fitness, a certain symmetry in that.

Ann was sitting on the bed making a thorough job of crying, chest heaving with sobs, tears pouring down her face to be mopped up with a soaked tissue. Walt was awake, staring and whimpering in his cot; Bill picked him up to comfort him and wondered how to comfort Ann.

'It's a long time ago, you know.'

'Not to me. Not to me. I wanted to see her!'

'Look . . .' But he didn't know what to say. He had a feeling of danger averted that he couldn't mention to her, couldn't tell her she might be better off . . . There was no comfort in that.

There was no comfort in anything. He got a box of tissues from the carryall and brought them to her.

'Did they say anything? How she died? When?'

'Nothing, I don't think they want to talk about it. It's kinder to leave it, I think.'

She nodded and began to dry her face. 'I want to go home.'

'Right. They'll understand. Take him, will you, while I fold the cot.'

He hoped she would find some comfort in holding Walt, but she took him as usual as if he were a parcel — fragile, but a parcel. Nothing had changed, except himself.

Ellen appeared at the door with a tray; a plate of sandwiches, a bottle of sherry and two glasses. She said soberly, full of respect for bereavement, 'She won't be wanting to come in to lunch. I'll bring coffee later.'

Ann called, 'Tell Aunt Em I'm sorry about the vase.'

'Oh, the vase. Don't worry about that. I was never so glad of anything in my life as to see that damned thing in pieces. Alice and Elaine can find something else to fight about.'

Later in the car Ann said sighing, 'Well, I've made my mark, got into the family history. I smashed the Sèvres vase.'

'As far as they are concerned, you never did a better thing.' He was awed by this; it was Sèvres, after all.

'They're trying to be kind.'

'I'm sure they meant it. And by the way, you didn't drop it. The old lady did.'

'I caused it. I gave her a shock.' Tears began to roll down her face again. 'She must have died in childbirth. That's why they won't tell me. Because I killed her.'

'Oh, for Christ's sake!' he thought, but paused before he objected. It was as good a story as any. It saw Nora safely stowed, out of reach of questions. He had had suicide in mind himself. He was glad she hadn't thought of that.

Finding words carefully, he said, 'Listen, Ann. You weren't born guilty. Nobody is born guilty. If your mother died in childbirth, you still didn't kill her. Newborn babies are not murderers, so don't be so bloody silly. And you didn't break the vase. And you're not guilty of being illegitimate, either.' Nor do you have to be the perfect plastic model of the perfect human being.

But he knew his words didn't reach her, would reach her

perhaps only after years of loving support.

His job for a lifetime. Not what he had intended. Not what he had intended at all.

In his own bed now, Gavin was dreaming.

There was a street light shining, bright and soft, liquid as a tear unshed in a bright eye, but without nimbus, confined to its globe by the blue half-light. Dawn or dusk? The clouds shone pink with the promise of morning. Out of sight, the ocean heaved a deep regular sigh, like a sleeping breath. The road was as white as white sand; under the street lamp it swerved; somewhere beyond, unseen it met the sea. Down the road the rats poured, a thick brown broth of rats bubbling; in all that multitude the light struck one eye only that shone like a ruby. The rats thudded past, swerved and were gone.

'At this stage,' said the lecturer's voice, solemn and resonant, 'flesh takes the appearance of spirit, thereby deceiving the cleverest of rats.'

Coming nearly to the surface, he cried, 'Bridie!'

'Mm? Yes? What's up?'

She came awake slowly, yawning.

'Don't you ever do that to me!'

'Do what?'

'Delude! Delude!'

Bridie settled again. 'But I'd never have to.'

That was all right then. Everything was all right. He went back to sleep.

ALSO BY AMY WITTING
I For Isobel

Born to a world without welcome, Isobel observes it as warily as an alien trying to pass for a native. Her collection of imaginary friends includes the Virgin Mary and Sherlock Holmes. Later on, she meets Byron, W.H. Auden and T.S. Eliot. She is not as much at ease with the flesh-and-blood people she meets, and least of all with herself, until a lucky encounter and a little detective work reveal her identity and her true situation in life.

'Isobel is instinctively searching for a lost part of her substance, the very memory of which has been obliterated. Prompted by her inexplicable sense of loss, she goes on her way, deviating, baffled, yet rejecting substitutes. To call the ending happy is to say both too much and too little. Was the lost part also searching for her? Amy Witting's admirers will find this novel as distinctive and compelling as her stories and poetry.'

Jessica Anderson

Broken Words   Helen Hodgman

Moss wants to go shopping.
Elvis wants an aquarium.
Harold wants to start his own religion.
Princess Anne might want to be left out of it.
Angst wants to know where his next meal is coming from.
Walter and Daphne want Rupert to wake up.
Manny, Maureen and Sue want to open a garage.
Beulah wants the Southern Belle.
Buster wants to take the baby to Berlin.
Hitler and the Bogeyman want only to be loved.
Le Professeur de Judo wants love to leave him alone.
Renate wants to know what love's got to do with it.
Hazel wants life to have a plot.
But you don't always get what you want . . .

'Helen Hodgman combines acute observation with a surreal imagination to give a stylishly bizarre account of the lives of a group of urban women now: *Broken Words* is funny and poignant, a vivid evocation of the cruelty and beauty of life' – *Shena Mackay*

Whatever Happened to Rosie Dunn?   Tom Beauford

For Sophie Parnell, private detective, the investigation into the death of her enigmatic cousin, daughter of a leading Sydney heart surgeon, takes her into a world of corruption and powerful people.

Following one lead after another she reaches a showdown in Thailand, confronting the evil mind behind the mystery – and faces the horror of what happened to Rosie Dunn.

Spidercup   Marion Halligan

Does a wife exist only when her husband is contemplating her? . . . A wife is called into being only by a husband; therefore does she cease to exist when he stops observing her, stops regarding her?

Elinor leaves her husband suddenly and goes to France, to the village of Sévérac-le-Château. There she ponders the lives of other women. In the seventeenth century a wife is murdered for faithlessness; in the early twentieth century a woman embroiders sheets for a trousseau never needed; in the 1980s a successful pediatrician may or may not know what her husband is up to.

Elinor's process of transformation – from a wife to a self – is written with subtlety and humour. The journey she undertakes is more than a journey of the flesh.

The Hanged Man in the Garden   Marion Halligan

'. . . the Hanged Man dangles gallantly by one foot and turning upside down observes the world. Its powers cannot harm him, he sees it clearly and afresh, all new. He is an individual. And he has a halo round his head.'

The Hanged Man represents a turn-around of perception that often occurs when an individual confronts pain. A baby dies, a husband is unfaithful, a woman spends a week in a cupboard, people strive to come to terms with grief and loss – variously they choose humour, despair, irony and hope. It is the unexpectedness of this illogical reversal that makes the experience precious. And, how ever hard life may be, the sensuous beauty of its surfaces is a source of pleasure.

One of Australia's foremost short-story writers, Marion Halligan explores, through the interweaving lives of a group of individuals, the complexities of pain.

PENGUIN - THE BEST AUSTRALIAN READING

Moonlight over the Estuary   Ken Methold

Moonlight over the Estuary is an hilarious account of one woman's search for love.

Rebecca Carmichael is the eternal optimist. She keeps hoping she will meet her knight in shining armour and be whisked away to a fairytale happy-ever-after ending of a kind she reads about in her favourite romantic fiction. As Rebecca falls in and out of love with some truly awful men she doesn't realise what she is missing while wearing her rose-coloured glasses.

Sister Kate   Jean Bedford

Kate Kelly grew up in a house of women: when the Kelly men were not in jail, they were outlaws. Kate's loyalty to her family becomes a bitter obsession.

Inevitably the police take brutal revenge on the Kelly Gang at Glenrowan. Kate must watch as the scorched body of her lover is strung up for public display. Neither wandering nor marriage, time nor drink, can blot out this gruesome climax to her young life.

Until the ashes of their heroism turn her mind to darkness.

PENGUIN - THE BEST AUSTRALIAN READING

The Glass Whittler   Stephanie Johnson

A young woman changes cities, but no one in the new city needs a glass whittler; Robyn, a single mother, buys a house on the proceeds of an unusual business; Nola is fat – one night, reminded of the joys of chocolate by the television she decides to go out – but Nola is locked inside her flat and cannot get out; a retired schoolmistress who has had a stroke is cared for by an alcoholic tramp who has made himself at home in her flat.

Twelve stories by a remarkable young writer. Stephanie Johnson writes about craving for love and companionship, for security and the approval of others. The people in these stories seem to find unusual ways of coping with the absurdities and constraints of modern life. But perhaps their solutions are not so strange.

Steel Beach   Margaret Barbalet

The view from the house distracted me from my work. Held between the beach and the escarpment, I would look up from my papers and my eye would take in the sweep of the coastline – the same coastline that Lawrence and Frieda had explored half a century before. Now I was the explorer, mapping out the life they had led there.

I met a surfer on the beach yesterday who was the image of Lawrence. As soon as I saw him, I knew he was important. He was my first clue.

BOOKS BY CRIENA ROHAN IN PENGUIN
The Delinquents

Brownie and Lola are young lovers in the 1950s – the age of the bodgie and widgie, imported American music, rock and roll – and a time when those who went their own way were considered to be 'delinquent'.

Despite attempts to separate them, they make their own life in the city, leaving Bundaberg far behind. In the world's view – that is, their mothers, welfare and the cops – they are unprepared for adult responsibilities. And even though the cops and welfare occasionally catch up, Lola and Brownie show they are capable of handling the world – a world to which they give a love and understanding that is rarely returned.

Down by the Dockside

Eilishe Cahaleen Deirdre Flynn, otherwise known as Lisha, is Australian by birth, Liverpool Irish in every other respect. Raised by her grandmother, she grows up in the tough slums of Port Melbourne during the Depression.

Swept away by the excitement and sleaziness of wartime Melbourne, Lisha marries a sailor at seventeen. By eighteen she is a mother, by twenty-one a widow. In desperation, she turns to the people of her childhood. She sings in night clubs, teaches in back-street dancing schools and associates with petty criminals.

PENGUIN - THE BEST AUSTRALIAN READING

BOOKS BY RUTH PARK IN PENGUIN
The Harp in the South

The Harp in the South is a nostalgic and moving portrait of the eventful family life of the Darcys, of Number Twelve-and-a Half Plymouth Street in Surry Hills, a Sydney slum. There grow the bitter-sweet first and last loves of Roie Darcy, who becomes a woman too quickly amid the brothels and the razor gangs, the tenaments and the sly-grog shops.

Poor Man's Orange

She knew the poor man's orange was hers, with its bitter rind, its paler flesh, and its stinging, exultant, unforgettable tang. So she would have it that way and wish it no other way. She knew that she was strong enough to bear whatever might come in her life as long as she had love.

In this poignant sequel to *The Harp in the South* Ruth Park tells of the Darcy family, and their vitality and humour in the midst of acute poverty.

Missus

Missus takes us behind the lives of Hughie and Mumma, out of the gritty realism of inner city slum life and into the past of the stations, the bush and the country towns. We meet them as they were in the early 1920s, drifter Hugh Darcy, the unwilling hero who sweeps the dreamily innocent Margaret Kilker off her feet. Ruth Park richly creates the turmoil of those early days of their courtship – in the dusty outback.

PENGUIN - THE BEST AUSTRALIAN READING

It's Raining in Mango   Thea Astley

Sometimes history repeats itself.

One family traced from the 1860s to the 1980s: from Cornelius to Connie to Reever, who was last seen heading north.

Cornelius Laffey, an Irish-born journalist, wrests his family from the easy living of nineteenth-century Sydney and takes them to Cooktown in northern Queensland where thousands of diggers are searching for gold in the mud. The family confront the horror of Aboriginal dispossession – Cornelius is sacked for reporting the slaughter. His daughter, Nadine, joins the singing whore on the barge and goes upstream, only to be washed out to sea.

The cycles of generations turn, one over the other. Only some things change. That world and this world both have their Catholic priests, their bigots, their radicals. Full of powerful and independent characters, this is an unforgettable tale of the other side of Australia's heritage.

Tirra Lirra by the River   Jessica Anderson

A beautifully written novel of a woman's seventy-year search to find a place where she truly belongs.

For Nora Porteous, life is a series of escapes. To escape her tightly knit small-town family, she marries, only to find herself confined again, this time in a stifling Sydney suburb with a selfish, sanctimonious husband. With a courage born of desperation and sustained by a spirited sense of humour, Nora travels to London, and it is there that she becomes the woman she wants to be. Or does she?